THE EBB TIDE

And Other Stories from Cornwall

THE EBB TIDE

And Other Stories from Cornwall

Edited by John T Wilson

Weavers Press Publishing

1991

First published in the UK by
Weavers Press Publishing
Tregeraint House
Zennor
Cornwall
TR26 3DB

British Library Cataloguing in Publication Data
The ebb tide and other stories from Cornwall.
I. Gribble, Gill
823.0108324237

ISBN 0-946017-22-0
ISBN 0-946017-23-9 pbk

Typeset by Bookman, 2c Merrywood Road, Bristol, BS3 1DX
Printed by Troutbeck Press, Antron Hill, Mabe, Penryn, Cornwall

Dedicated to all those who love Cornwall and especially Cornwall's writers

The title story is dedicated by the author to Stella

ACKNOWLEDGEMENTS

Lucy Spear's story 'At the Bottom of the Garden' was first published in 'Fear' magazine.

CONTENTS

PREFACE

This book of Cornish stories came into being as the result of my experiences in teaching creative writing in Cornwall both for the WEA in Newquay, Redruth and Camborne and for the Falmouth Adult Education Centre. I discovered that in Cornwall, as elsewhere, there were a number of new writers, sometimes unaware of their talents, writing short stories which cried out to be published. Some of those writers are here along with those others in the collection whose stories also caught my imagination. My definition of Cornish stories was that they should be by Cornish people or those living in Cornwall or that the stories themselves should have a Cornish connection or setting. I hope you enjoy them as much as I have enjoyed putting the collection together.

John T Wilson
Editor

INTRODUCTION

Cornwall is famous for its stories – smugglers, giants, valour on the sea, piskeys and mermaids. You will find none of them here.

What you will find is new stories by writers who show a Cornwall as dark and mysterious, as human and touching, as strange and wonderful and as humorous as those tales of bygone times.

What makes a good story? One of the great storytellers from the past, Sir Philip Sidney, described the successful story as "a speaking picture, teaching with delight." It comes alive and, more than this, it has something to say.

He also said that a good storyteller "cometh unto you with a tale which holdeth children from play and old men from the chimney corner."

I think you will find that all the stories in this collection which I have had the pleasure of putting together for your enjoyment will paint just that kind of vivid picture, grabbing your imagination and delighting you with their power to make you think – sometimes strange new thoughts. Good stories will tell you things about yourself that you did not even suspect. They have the power to shock, to surprise and to delight. Some of these Cornish stories will do all three.

The tales here are varied. Some are humorous, like the irrepressible Gladys Harvey's 'It's Travel that Broadens the Mind' or 'Bella Vista' by Roy Phillips, first winner of the TSB Peninsula Prize, with his delightful novel 'The Saffron Eaters'. One or two are set in the past but most, despite being set in modern times, explore the dark side of life which seems to lie just beneath the surface of Cornish life and landscape.

Babies under gooseberry bushes, retired spinsters sparring with gossip in a genteel home, Dads and Mums, foxes and fighters, love and death, marriage and murder – it's all here, life in the raw. Read it, taste it, feel it. Pick it up and start and you won't be able to put it down till you reach the satisfying climax of Doreen Fiol's moving tale of a father who once nearly taught his daughter to fly – "Look at Me Daddy – I'm Flying."

'THE EBB TIDE AND OTHER STORIES FROM CORNWALL' is the first in a series of Cornish short stories Weavers Press hope to publish in the future.

THE EBB TIDE

BY GILL GRIBBLE

I watched, silently, as the yellow circle appeared in the mirror below the test-tube. It didn't go away. How long had it been? I'd almost lost count. Thirty-two months, one for each year of my life. Somehow the correlation seemed quite fair, and, in reality, the weeks had passed in such a way that I'd always believed one day they would come to an end.

I smoothed my hands slowly over my stomach and glancing across the room at my reflection was surprised to find that I didn't look any different. My eyes roamed up and down my outline until they were drawn to a place above my head, where a dried flower headdress hung on the wall, beside a framed photograph. I'd chosen big daisies. He loves me, he loves me not. I could smell the soft grass on the steep slope behind the tennis court, as Jennifer sat plucking the petals and casting them to the wind, while we waited anxiously for the outcome. Why didn't he ever love me? They giggled at me every time. Suddenly Jennifer pulled at my hand.

"I've got a better idea. We went to the fair on Saturday and Mummy saw a gypsy who read her palm. You do it like this". She studied the thin lines meandering across my hand, pretending not to notice the dirt and smudges of ink. "Well, that's a surprise! You're going to get married! Look, these lines join up to make an 'M'. But that's not all. Give me your wrist". She shoved my cuff roughly out of the way. "Oh, too bad! Look, girls. Dear Jinnie isn't going to have any children. There aren't any lines around her wrist. What a shame! I'm going to marry someone rich and have hundreds of babies. Look!" She pushed her hand under my nose.

"I don't care," I said, tossing my head so they wouldn't see the tears. "I don't want babies anyway. I'm going to do something important with my life."

They were roaring like hyenas as I stumbled away. Why wasn't Helen ever here when I needed her? I ran around the corner hardly able to see and bumped into her. She hugged her arms around me.

"Oh Helen, they're such a rotten bunch," I cried.

"Don't listen to them, Jin. They don't know a thing. They just don't know a thing".

I was grinning like a Cheshire cat. If you could see me now, Jennifer Richards, you'd–

Suddenly the door clicked open. I turned round and tried to hide the huge chest of drawers with my small body.

Julian frowned.

"What are you doing?"

"Nothing."

He laughed. "Nothing, huh?"

"It's just . . . well I didn't want to say anything until I was sure. I couldn't let us raise our hopes."

He moved me gently aside and stared at the containers, "How long overdue are you?"

"Three weeks."

"Three weeks! God, how have you kept quiet for so long?"

I couldn't answer. The tears came quickly as I laid my head on his shoulder. We wept together then, each of us sharing the other's relief.

"When are you going to tell Helen?" he asked, wiping his cheek with his sleeve.

"Later on. Maybe tomorrow." My voice was still shaky.

"Why not now?" he said, "Go on, tell her now."

I knew what Helen would be doing. She would be curled up on her sofa, wearing something beautifully tailored and creaseless, listening to either the Stranglers or Mahler. That's how it was with her. I could remember so clearly the night we saw the Stranglers at the Fiesta back in '78. We'd been given free tickets by a roadie friend and had gone along for a laugh. Helen hadn't minded being the only one not wearing black plastic or a safety pin. Yet she fell in love with the music immediately. I wondered which pulsing bass line the telephone would interrupt.

"Hello?"

"Hello. Helen . . ."

"Wait a minute." She disappeared for a moment. "Hi."

"Helen?"

"What?" Her voice had a hint of impatience.

"How would you like to be an honorary Auntie?" I asked.

"Oh bloody Hell, Jin, not the gerbil again! Can't you get it seen to or something?"

"Helen, it's– "

"Damned irresponsible, if you ask me!" she interrupted.

"No, Helen. It's me. Listen. I'm pregnant." I heard her cough, pretend to clear her throat, and then suddenly she gave up and started to sob.

The weeds between the rows of carrots had proved particularly stubborn. I'd also found some large brambles hiding at the base of the wall that hadn't come out cleanly. As I bent over to get my breath back, I felt a wave of nausea and I knew that I was going to be sick. I managed to get out into the lane before the muscle spasms took over. Some shiny polished feet stood beside me.

"Charming way to greet your long lost friends. Maybe I'll go away again."

"Perhaps you should have told me you were coming," I grinned. Helen placed her arm around my shoulder and led me back into the garden. After telling me off like a little child she went on to describe the weeks she'd spent in Chartres and Paris. As she spoke I closed my eyes and tried to imagine the fabulous stained glass, the smoky blue watercolours, the geometrical flowers. I could smell the air inside the museums, feel the warm darkness of the tiny bookshop she'd discovered squeezed in beside a cafe in the Rue de Saintonge.

"Have you got a birth plan?" she demanded.

"A what?" I couldn't see the connection with fine art or literature. But I should have seen it coming.

"Look, it's really important that you state very clearly what you want as early as possible. Otherwise they just do what they have to do in order to fit in with everything else. I've been doing some background reading because I knew you wouldn't bother." In truth, dear Helen, I hadn't dared to believe that I was actually going to give birth.

"You must understand," she continued, "that this has got to be a wonderful experience for you and the baby. And it will be, if you know what you want and how to get it. After all, you may not get another chance."

She was right, there. And, give her her due, she appeared to have studied the subject carefully in her consideration for us.

She grabbed my hand. "Better still, why not have a home birth? I could be there to hold your hand."

"You!" I exclaimed, immediately regretting it. "Wouldn't you be embarrassed?"

"Oh come off it," she said, "we've known each other far too long for any of that."

"Well anyway," I protested, "I couldn't. I'm already booked into hospital, and with my gynaecological history it's probably the best place to be."

"Best for who?" she interrupted. "The staff, or you and your baby? Look, I'm sorry, I'm not against hospitals at all. I just feel that with you being you, potentially having to fight for what you want isn't going to be very relaxing. Of course, you could get on marvellously with the people around you. But then again, you might not."

"I'm not sure either of us is really experienced enough to discuss such matters," I teased.

"Bet Jennifer is by now!" she laughed. "Shall we try to find out?"

"Over my dead body!" We were both laughing. But suddenly I stopped smiling. I should have said "our" not "my". For if I died now, or even tomorrow, there would be two of us, hand bound in hand, travelling along the darkened tunnel towards the opalescent light beyond. I would have to take it with me. It? How could I use such a word in connection with a person who already had a pattern of characteristics that would be uniquely hers? We could have two hundred children and every one would be different. Like the other one. There had been one other, at least I believed there had. The hospital thought so too, to begin with. But after a barrage of tests and days kept shut up like a lunatic they concluded that I was merely suffering from a half blocked maternal instinct and that my best option was to go home and send the white fluffy bootees to the Save the Children shop and get on with the rest of my life.

I looked up and saw that Helen was studying my face.

"You always drift back to then, don't you?" she asked.

"I shouldn't need to now, should I?" I answered. I patted my stomach. "Not bad for an old crank who's only firing on one cylinder."

Julian appeared, his hands smeared with earth. "Like a cup of tea, Hel?"

"No thanks, I've got to go. Oh!" She rummaged in the bottom of her enormous carpet bag. "I nearly forgot. I brought you a present." She handed over a square brown parcel, kissed me on the cheek and was gone. Julian went back to the lengths of twine and pegs of wood he was carefully setting out. His was a very ordered world. Vegetables grew at precise intervals in ramrod-straight rows. Babies were born in sparklingly clean hospitals, wrapped in white gowns, lined up in perspex boxes. They didn't pop out on the back seats of cars, in bus shelters, or the cosy confines of one's own front room. I had started to warm to the seeds of ideas that Helen had sown, but I knew that even if I formulated a plan, I would have to work hard to persuade Julian. It was something I hadn't considered before.

"Aren't you going to open it?" Julian asked. I'd forgotten all about Helen's gift. Nearly all of the books were in French but the photographs spoke for themselves. Grainy black and white images of curled up faces and wrinkled fingers nestling softly on their mother's breast. Some of the babies were floating in water, their tongues tasting, eyes wide. The most startling aspect of them all was the atmosphere of total peace. I became aware of Julian breathing over my shoulder.

"Why have you got these?" he asked.

"I don't really know. I think Helen thought we might be interested," I answered. He shrugged his shoulders and went indoors. I picked up the handles of the wheelbarrow and pushed it down the lane, and as we bumped along over the ruts the sun flashed off the roof of the greenhouse. The sky was turning deep orange and in the air was the tang of impending rain.

I was walking across a bridge which started to rise higher above the water. I couldn't see the land any more, only masses of blue sky, when suddenly the bridge ended and I was falling a long, long way, until I hit the surface of the water. Now I was descending more slowly, but still going down, very aware of the density of the water, the increasing pressure on my chest and a burning pain in my belly. I was fighting to breathe and had just reached the turning point when my stomach ripped open and the baby burst out. Only when I looked down, it wasn't a baby at all, but a green, writhing creature with a gaping mouth full of needle sharp teeth.

That's it, I've had enough. I turned over and felt for the warm smooth curve of Julian's shoulder. There was a dull ache in the small of my back which spread around towards the sides. I'd been sweating with the fear and felt very cold. I pulled my nightie down around my thighs to get warm and when my hands reappeared from under the covers I saw that they were streaked with red.

I lay as still as I possibly could. I love you, already. I love you too much to let you go. Just hold on tight, babe, and we'll be alright.

The midwife gazed sideways as she listened through the stethoscope. Her hands were surprisingly hot as she carefully palpated my abdomen, chatting away in her mild Dublin voice. "Sure, I think you'll be O.K., Just have to take it a bit easier for a while."

"I guess now isn't the time to mention that I'd been considering the possibility of a home birth?" I said. Her glasses slipped on her nose.

"Probably not," she answered. "But if you're a good girlie and things go well, we might be able to look into it." She leaned closer. "Actually, to tell the truth, I love doing them." Well that's a good start, I thought. Two or three down and only one to go.

It felt strange, watching Helen help with the digging, getting dirt under her finger nails, whilst I sat like a contented cat, basking in the sun. The baby seemed to have noticed the weather too, and had begun kicking in earnest. Impatiently I wished I could peep through my navel like a spy-hole in a door and see who was inside, what colour eyes they had, what type of nose. But then, having waited so long, a few months more would be nothing.

Julian was impressed with Helen's application to these new tasks. She'd worked as hard as him on a day which was too hot for such exertion. I wandered into the kitchen and brought out a tray of cool drinks.

"Wonderful!" Helen exclaimed. "Ice cubes, too! You'd better start stocking your freezer. We might need a few to soothe your fevered brow when baby comes."

"Wouldn't they melt on the way to the hospital?" Julian asked. Helen looked at me, but I couldn't meet her eyes.

"Not if we weren't going there," she said.

"How do you mean?" he demanded.

"Well, we were thinking, I mean Jinnie was thinking about maybe having the baby at home." I could hear crickets in the grass, and birdsong from beyond the hedge. But not a word from Julian. He just stared at me, a look of disbelief on his face.

"Thanks for letting me know. You might even invite me," he finally said, gathering up some tools, and walking off to the shed. Helen was more surprised than me. She had thought that this might be a good time to introduce the idea, with all of us together. But we realised, then, that we hadn't got the measure of his protectiveness towards our unborn child.

I had to find a way of tackling the subject, of sorting out our hopes and aspirations so that we knew where we stood. We were travelling on a journey of finite length whose outcome was predictable, yet we still had differing opinions as to how that might be achieved.

"Talk to me," I begged.

"What about?"

"Us. You. Me. Our child. Don't just go silent on me."

"It seems to me that you decide things with Helen, not me. She has a strong influence on you."

"She's a good friend. I respect what she says. But now I'm talking about the three of us. You and me and our baby. Like any woman, I want the best for all of us. And I think that having the baby here could give us the chance of a good beginning." I could see that at least he was listening.

"But what about the risks?" he said.

"Statistics show– "

"Sod the statistics!" he shouted. "We've waited too long for this and can't afford to take chances. What does your midwife feel about all this – especially after– "

"Actually, she's quite in favour. I'm healthy now and so is the baby." I went over to him and held his hands. "This means such a lot to me. I just want to try. Please let me try."

We stood looking at each other for some time. "Well, at the end of the day I suppose it's really up to you. You're the one who's got to go through with it all," he said.

I love you. Please let it be good, let us be happy, let our baby be safe.

Helen stood wobbling on the chair, her arms high above her head. "Like this?" she asked.

"No, over a bit. Yes, that's better."

"Are you sure the baby's going to appreciate all this?" she said.

"Of course," I answered, "As long as it arrives before Twelfth Night." I picked the straw angels out of the box and added them to the tree, which was already groaning under the weight of coloured tinsel, baubles, and small parcels. What a beautiful world for a first glimpse.

"When are you collecting the tub?" Helen said.

"Next week, I think."

"Has he come round to the idea of the water birth?" she asked.

"He just feels glad to have the opportunity to be more involved," I answered. Since we had graduated to the possibility of the baby being born underwater we had given Julian the chance to put his practical skills to great use. The tap and hose connections had been checked, the water heater timed, the logs stacked beside the fire. We had had to rearrange the furniture which gave the house an atmosphere of expectance, as if a party were about to begin. We're ready now. All we need is our guest of honour. But let's just get past Christmas and not interrupt the festivities.

By the New Year it had turned bitterly cold with some fierce winds. I felt safer indoors, less likely to succumb to gravity. I paced up and down the lounge, stopping occasionally to try to shift the baby's head which was pressing on my sciatic nerve. I glanced at my watch and Julian noticed.

"Are you O.K.?" he asked.

"Fine," I lied. Twelve minutes. That one was quicker. I leaned on one leg and rubbed my back.

"Shouldn't you get hold of Helen now?" I looked at my watch again.

"Yes, I guess you're right." I dialled her number. "Would you like to come over?" I asked.

"Brilliant!" she laughed, "I can get out of the washing up."

I felt like a castaway, drifting helplessly on a strong tide, with Julian and Helen as the islands I was struggling to reach. Just as I got near, I would be dragged away again by another contraction, to disappear into that dark red whorl of pain which I knew I mustn't fight. The warm water slopped around my belly as I sat up or kneeled down, dealing with each one as it came. As a huge contraction shuddered through my body, there was a blinding flash of lightning followed by a single thunderous crack. And then, she emerged from her safe, secure swimming pool, through the waters of the tub, and up to the conscious touch of our waiting hands. There was complete silence as we all waited in awe for her to voice her hellos.

"The camera," Julian whispered. "Helen, the camera."

"I can't," she croaked, as the tears poured down her face. I lay back in the water and held our daughter's wrinkled body close to mine and felt not love, not the instant love I had imagined, but the powerful emotions of a mortal puzzle which had just begun. I wondered if we might solve it.

We were floating, in time, in space, through reality toward dreams and back. As we drifted into reality again, I saw the midwife fix the clamps, offer Julian the scissors and he cut the cord. Now we were three.

A few hours later, tired but wide awake, I placed her tiny pink form on my chest and felt her heart beating as she drifted to sleep. We had a daughter. A perfect human being. We had counted the fingers and toes ourselves.

Julian opened his eyes. "Morning, Mum, alright?"

"Yes, fine, I feel quite bright."

"How's Ruby?" he asked. "Did she feed?"

"Of course," I said. "She's asleep now, though."

"You were wonderful last night. Both of you. It's not easy to say, but I'm very glad that you did what you did." He reached over and turned on the radio, which was barely audible. "Listen," he said, "It's quite interesting. They're talking about last night's brief storm, because it seems that the engine house at Pool was struck by a thunderbolt, and the stack has been destroyed. Bet Ruby did it! She's a powerful little lady, you know."

"Don't be silly," I replied, "How could she?" But I wasn't convinced by my reply. Perhaps there were forces that we couldn't comprehend. I turned over and gazed at her soft sleeping face, the pale curve of her cheek, the minute eyelashes sweeping upwards. Her hand jerked involuntarily and brushed her head. She stirred and opened her unfocussed eyes, looking towards me as though she could not only see me, but beyond me into far deeper places. How would I find the necessary strength to love and protect this person for the rest of her life?

Julian's voice pushed in between us. "We'll stay at home today, just the three of us, cosy and snug. Then perhaps tomorrow we might venture out and see some of the world."

When tomorrow came, it was still and warm and bright. With little more than Ruby's nose peeping out from the winter garments we walked up the hill. The engine house was surrounded by scaffolding as skilled workmen began rebuilding the damaged chimney. Julian whispered underneath the white woolly hat. "Look, Ruby, you did that!" Glancing up at me he added, "Why don't we catch the bus and go and register her birth?"

We sat quietly in the dark, musty office, looking at the multicoloured bird posters which obscured the walls whilst the registrar carefully prepared his papers.

"Now tell me," he began, smiling as he peered over the top of his glasses, "was this little miss born at home by accident – or by design?"

"Oh, by design," we said together, refraining from discussing her less conventional arrival. He looked amused.

"Well, all I can say," he continued, "is that I'm glad it wasn't in foreign parts. You know, over The Bridge." He chuckled away to himself. "In which case," he added, as he painstakingly assembled a gold fountain pen, "I'd better do my best writing for this young Cornish lady." And all the while he chatted on as his weathered old hands made the shapes of his beautiful flowing script.

We took the birth certificates and folded them into the envelope. Now it was official. Now it was real. We were parents and would remain so for the rest of our lives.

In the middle of the night any sense of reality lay hidden outside the thick bedroom curtains. I would be woken by the furious kicking of small feet in my back, by the sucking sounds of a tight fist pressed into a hungry mouth. She lay between us, her dark eyes twinkling and beady like a squirrel's in the half light. Once satiated, she would soon sleep again. But as her rib cage sighed up and down, I would lie awake, just watching, for hours, nurturing the love which had seeped into me, slowly at first, yet unavoidably.

"I love you." Julian's voice woke me. "You're so clever to have such a pretty baby. Everyone says how beautiful she is. She has such gorgeous brown eyes."

"Well, she got those from you, not me."

"Great!" he laughed, "Was that my only contribution?"

I thought about the sleeping face lying flat against the sheet. What contribution had I made? Was her sucked-in mouth a little like mine? Or was she just herself, a unique individual who had merely borrowed my body for a while in order to strengthen her own in readiness for her discoveries? Perhaps she would become organised and purposeful like her father. Or maybe she would drift along with her head in the clouds, popping down from time to time to snatch at an idea or two. Either way, we were bound to love her, for herself, and what that might be. Which day had her heart begun beating? Maybe it was at night. Maybe it was the time when she almost slipped out of our hands, had made us gasp at our complacency. I tried to look at her without these complications but emotions got in the way.

"Julian?"

"Mmmm?"

"Do you love Ruby?" I asked.

"Of course," he answered quickly, "What a daft question." He shuffled down under the covers and, wrapping his arm around our daughter as if to prove his point, settled down to doze.

"Do you think it's possible to love someone too much?" I didn't wait for an answer. "It's just that sometimes I feel that I love her so much that it's as if I'm being strangled. It's as though she's trying to suffocate me through the power of my love for her. She's too perfect, too pretty, it makes me feel totally inadequate, completely incapable of caring for such a flawless being."

"You think too much," he said. "All new mothers have feelings like that from time to time. Why look for problems that aren't there?" He sounded like a page from another nameless babycare book. Perhaps it was true, but I was beginning to be afraid.

The following day he returned to work. I wasn't prepared for the loneliness which came along and hung around me like a huge thundercloud, forcing me to stay in bed. I didn't get up until lunchtime, and even then it was only Ruby who was hungry. With the second post came a glossy postcard of the Madonna and Child, smiling serenely, oblivious, like its sender.

My own child had found her lungs and unlike her painted counterpart had screwed up her face which was now a deep scarlet, as she bellowed with rage or pain, I didn't know which. Trying to feed her partly muffled the sound but was obviously not the solution. I walked around, sat down, laid her across my knee, over my shoulder, as I willed the clock to speed up. I didn't hear Julian come home. He took her from my arms and walked up and down the stairs, bobbing her about with each step. She responded quickly to the rhythmic movements and sighing repeatedly, fell asleep.

"Who taught you that one?" I asked.

"I don't know," he answered, "Maybe I'm just a natural."

"Well I'm off to bed, then," I said. "Wasn't much point getting up today."

"What's the matter?" he said.

"Nothing," I muttered, "Just nothing."

The crocuses and narcissi were stretching out of the window box towards the Spring sunshine when Helen appeared again at our door. The wanderer returned. Could one have a prodigal friend?

She scooped up Ruby and cooed at her. "Oh Jin!" she exclaimed, "she's so pretty! She's got eyes just like Smarties. I can honestly say I've never seen such a beautiful baby. You're very lucky."

I looked away as the tears gathered around my eyes, silently rolling down my cheeks. We hadn't chosen a perfect baby. She should've been someone else's. Why was this so much harder than I had imagined?

"Happy Mother's Day!" Julian said. A precarious breakfast tray preceded him into the room. In the middle of the tray, a vase of daffodils was lit by a shaft of sunlight that had arrived uninvited through the window.

"What would you like to do today?" he asked. "It's your day, you can choose whatever you like."

I thought for a moment. "Just to begin with," I said, "I think I'd like to go off with Ruby on my own."

"Sure," he replied, "I'll see you both later on then."

As we went out, wrapped well against the cold air, Julian pushed a single daffodil into my coat buttonhole. "Have a nice day, SuperMum," he grinned, "Take care of our special waterbaby."

Roadworks in the centre of town sent us driving along the road which wound its way through endless terraces of stone houses until they petered out and lumpy ploughed fields appeared. Ruby stared intently at the passing hedges, where new green leaves waved and stirred. Occasionally a seagull flew overhead, attracted by the newly turned earth, circling to follow a relentless tractor. Soon there were more gulls as we came nearer to the coast. The road flattened out onto the peninsula, marked out by brown patches of barren land dotted here and there with small twisted bushes. In the distance I could make out the twinkling of the sea, playing hide-and-seek behind the headland, and as we overtook a silage load, we cut across to the right and on to the road which led to the cove.

The way was punctuated with jagged fingers of lichen-painted granite, sticking out of rounded clumps of heather like mystical signposts. But which way were they pointing? Out of the car, I tucked Ruby firmly inside my coat, and walked down the shelving path which wound its way to the floor of the valley and the cove beyond. Once or twice, my feet slid on the stony surface, but I held on tightly to my precious bundle. As we climbed down the steps the noise of the waves grew louder, loud enough to welcome us in spite of the calm weather. I chose my route over the massive serpentine boulders until we were face to face with the sea and, slipping Ruby out from under my coat, I held her at arms length towards the gentle spray. Her legs swung wildly with delight as she watched the waves roll, one after another, to break ahead against the solid masses. She knows. She knows that you are perfection, the faultless, powerful one. That I am the flawed and weak. I turned, and choosing a flat rock, I laid her down and began to undress her. Her smile was unchanging as her silken skin absorbed the cool breeze. As though handling a porcelain doll, I carried her to a deep patch of water, where my hands, detached from the rest of my body, gently laid her down. I saw my fingers slip away, release their hold, saw those gorgeous eyes sparkle as they swam beneath the surface. There was no sound. My palms turned towards the sky and followed me to rest against an enormous blue-green rock streaked with yellow and red. As the damp coldness penetrated my awareness, my head drooped to touch the powdery petals of the daffodil in my coat. I sat, eyes closed, and waited for the peace, the overwhelming peace, which I knew would tell me that the sea had taken her back.

Drowning

BY GARY COUZENS

Blue, deep blue, my sister's eyes. I stare down into them, anxious for a glimmer of recognition.

"Beatrice?" I say. "It's me. Maria."

She gazes up at me from the hospital bed. I squeeze her hand. And remember.

Blue, deep blue, my sister's eyes. Her eighteen-year-old face, reflected in her dressing-table mirror, rapt in concentration as she leans forward, applying mascara. A tumble of Titian curls framing a long Modigliani face. There's something haughty about her as she pouts her lips to receive their offering of lipstick. Imperious beauty. Golden girl. Fallen angel.

"Beatrice . . .?" I say.

"Mmmm?" she answers, as she zips up her mid-length skirt.

"Is it Dave?"

"Yeah, it's Dave." Her answer is offhand, as if she knows already that Dave, her latest boyfriend, will be a minor character in the drama of her life.

Blue, deep blue, my sister's eyes. And beside them my own, nondescript brown. We're twins, but there's no resemblance. She's some maverick dredged up from our family's gene pool; one might suspect she isn't my father's child. But I am her twin, and clearly of my father's stock. Age me thirty years and I could be my aunt Celia, flat-faced plain, greying hair scraped back from her forehead, fumbling with rosary beads. Years of marital domination left a void behind at her husband's death. A worst-case scenario made flesh.

Now I sit by Beatrice's bed, holding her hand. Her skin is naturally fair, paled further by the greenish fluorescent lights. Her hair is shorter now, collar-length. When she was younger it went down to the middle of her back, devil may care; now, at age thirty, it's shorter to denote maturity, responsibility.

She squeezes my hand.

"Oh, thank God," I say.

The next day I discharge Beatrice from hospital. We take the Underground first back to her flat to collect some clothes and toiletries and then on to Paddington.

She shields her eyes from the sun with her hand. A bright day, and her eyes, even behind glasses, can't take the onslaught. Slender, deceptively frail-looking in a plain yellow top and long thin floral-print skirt, she seems very vulnerable, holding on to me as we're buffeted by the aimless crush of the Tube crowd.

Questions hang in the air. No doubt she'll answer them as best she can. I know facts if not reasons. First there was the phone call.

"Could I speak to Mrs Maria Grant, please?" A distant male voice crackling at the end of the line.

"Speaking."

"I've, er, got bad news about your sister."

I go cold. "What is it? What's happened?"

"Yes, er . . . Miss Andrews was admitted to hospital this morning. She took some sleeping pills. Her condition is stable. As the next of kin, we had to let you know."

"Thank you. I'll come immediately."

I make quick arrangements for someone to collect and look after James, my son, then I drive to Bodmin and take the Intercity to London. It's a journey of an hour and three quarters and I spend it gazing out of the window, unable to read my paper or do anything but think of what Beatrice has done. As I get off at Paddington I'm at first disorientated – a mass of people milling about, held in by the walls, the high arched roof – that I clutch my handbag to myself, holding myself in, protecting. The sheer noise – a thousand people talking, shouting, the tannoy booming out announcements – overwhelms my eardrums. It's years since I've been to London, first time since I moved to Cornwall, that I feel like a little girl again, alone, lost and afraid.

I discover a little more at the hospital. It was Beatrice herself who dialled 999, and gave her name and address before losing consciousness. The ambulance staff arrived to find the door unlocked.

Facts. As to reasons, only Beatrice can tell me.

Blue, deep blue, my sister's eyes. Often they flash with contempt, an implacable *no*. Everything she does is in reaction to me; if not me, then to our father. I'm the studious one, she the rebel; I'm the kind of pupil the teachers take pride in while despairing of her. And of course the comparisons exacerbate the tension. Were we not conceived at the same time, carried in the same womb, born within minutes of each other, there wouldn't be that incessant making of examples.

And over the years her reaction against me continues. I'm the one who married, settled down, had a child; the fact that I'm divorced is irrelevant to this scheme. On the other hand, she's never married, just had a succession of lovers.

Eighteen years old, I lie on my bed, listening to Beatrice and my father argue. Their voices are low, but they carry through the ceiling to my room above.

"You are not to stay out till all hours," says our father. "You're far too young."

"I'm old enough. I can do what I like."

"When you're living in my house, young lady, you'll do what I say. When you're living on your own I don't give a damn what you do. Are you sleeping with this boy?"

"What's it to you?"

"I'm not having my daughter sleeping around."

"I do *not* sleep around!"

"Why can't you be more like your sister?"

That question. Asked many times, in many forms. And when not asked out loud, tacit.

On the train journey home Beatrice says little. She watches the countryside go past and smokes one cigarette after another. I try to hold a conversation but after a while I give up and read the magazine I bought at Paddington.

Back in Bodmin I drive to James's school to pick him up. Although I spoke to him on the phone from the hospital last night, I'm anxious to see him again; I feel half missing if he's not there. My son. Six years old.

"Won't be a minute," I say as I get out of the car. Beatrice nods. As I walk away I glance back at her, face greyed by the reflections on the window, chin in palm, fingers obscuring her mouth. I flash a quick smile.

It begins to rain as I cross the road; fat single drops spatter on my coat. I walk over to where James stands, under shelter with his class teacher.

"Hello, Mrs Grant," she says.

"Sorry I'm late," I say. "I've just got back from the station, picking up my sister."

"That's okay," she says and smiles. "James has been very good."

"Makes a change," I say. James grins up at me. "Come on, trouble," I say and take his hand and cross the road again.

"Hello, James," says Beatrice as I let him in.

"Hello, Auntie Beatrice." He's picking up a definite Cornish accent, I notice. From his surroundings: he was born here in Bodmin. I was pregnant with him when my husband and I moved to this area. His voice makes a striking contrast with the Received Pronunciation Beatrice and I speak.

"Your aunt's come to stay for a little while," I say.

And Beatrice smiles, for the first time today. There's an affection between aunt and nephew that I hope will help her through. With a child's unselfconsciousness James might stand a better chance of reaching her than I might.

I put James to bed at half past eight then come back downstairs. Beatrice is in the kitchen, reheating the kettle for another coffee. The fluorescent light does her no favours. She seems older now all of a sudden, with a wide-eyed, over-awake look. Underweight. I realise how much she has been living on nerve-ends, coffee and cigarettes. Her nails are bitten. She has said she doesn't sleep well, and all that caffeine can't be helping.

We go back into the lounge. I sit on a chair, gathering up my legs under me, tugging at the hem of the long loose Laura Ashley dress I've changed into; she sits opposite me, legs set square, the coffee cup held on her knees. About five cigarette butts lie curled and grey in the ashtray in front of her.

"You realise," I say, "you're welcome to stay as long as you like. As long as you need."

She nods. "Yes. I'm very grateful to you, Maria."

"Oh, it's nothing," I say, waving my hand. "What about your job?"

"That's okay. I'll call in sick on Monday." She puts the coffee cup down on a coaster. "Now, if I'm not being too rude, I'd like to go to bed."

"No, no. Sleep's a great healer." I lead her down the hall to the spare room where I've made up a bed for her.

I move to go, but she makes a sound which stops me. I turn and suddenly she embraces me. "See you tomorrow," she whispers.

"We can talk a lot," I say.

I watch her go into her room, shut the door. Silence. I gaze at the door for a while, but it yields nothing. I turn on my heel and walk back to the lounge.

Coffee-cup in hand, I gaze out of the window at the darkened garden, the silent roads. Penny, my cat, winds herself about my legs, then jumps up onto the windowsill; absently, I scratch her behind the ear as I continue to look out. She rubs herself against the top of my thigh.

I think of Mark, my husband, again; I now do so, so rarely that when I do I surprise myself at it. It's now two years since he left me, saying that he wanted a change, I was cold, I didn't offer myself, didn't give anything. Perhaps I didn't, or perhaps it was simply that the love had died. We married too early, straight after graduation, and we've both changed in the meantime. I wonder how he is now; I see him rarely. I've seen a few men since then, but nothing has lasted. The presence of a young child has tended to act as a deterrent. Not that I mind: although sex is a great pleasure, it's not something I can't live without.

If I have not given much before, I have to now. For my sister's sake, at least.

Blue, deep blue, my sister's eyes. Distorted by tears as she stands at our father's graveside. I hold her hand as the coffin is lowered into the ground. Those around us – Mark; Beatrice's then boyfriend – stand back, leaving us to our grief. Her hand is held up to her face as she sobs. Tears do not flow freely: they catch in her, and she trembles as they work themselves loose.

She was never close to her father; they were often in conflict. So why does she cry now, and so painfully? Perhaps there was affection there, a grudging one born of respect for the opponent. Or maybe she is crying for herself, a lost soul with no-one to react against.

In the morning I serve Beatrice breakfast in bed and sit on the counterpane as she eats.

"Slept well?" I say.

"Mmm," she says nodding, mouth full of cornflakes. She sits up in bed, in a borrowed nightdress. It's loose on her, her small breasts hanging free as she leans forward. Penny has followed me in and sits purring on my lap, warm even through the padding of my dressing-gown.

"Anyway, get up in your own time," I say. "It's going to be a lovely day. We can take a walk, the three of us."

"Yes, I'd like that. Thank you very much."

After breakfast we walk down the lane to the village. Overhanging trees splinter the light; a high hedge on our right encloses a field. James runs on ahead leaving Beatrice and I to walk arm in arm. We could grow old like this, I think.

"This is wonderful," says Beatrice. "I'm envious."

"Mark and I set our hearts on living in the country," I say. "We couldn't wait to get away from the town."

"I'm a townie," says Beatrice, lighting a cigarette. "But it certainly makes a pleasant change. It's so peaceful. I can't get over the three-digit phone numbers. Progress hasn't got this far."

A pleasant change. It's said with a little too much edge, too much knowing irony, to be unselfconscious. A pleasant change from what? Although I didn't witness the scene, I see her collapsed on the floor of her flat, trying to vomit up the pills she swallowed, calling the ambulance before she blacked out.

"Do you still see Mark, Maria?"

I shake my head. "He's moved away now. He's got married again. Since he doesn't support me, he doesn't have any reason to involve himself with me too much. I just get letters now and again, holiday postcards, birthday and Christmas cards, and presents for James. That's all."

"Do you plan to marry again?"

I shrug. "I may do, I may not. Who knows? There's no-one in the offing."

A pause, then she says: "You know, I envy you, Maria."

"Envy me? How come?"

"You've got your act together."

I laugh.

She looks hurt. "What's so funny?"

"I just feel all I've done is what's expected of me. I've played safe every inch of the way. I've never gone for broke, never taken risks . . ."

"Yes, but you're secure. Organised. I never am. I just go from one chaos to another. Just as if I've never stopped being a student, really."

"How do you mean?"

"Well, staying up late and going in early. Drinking, smoking, sleeping around and getting hurt. Did you know I had an abortion once?"

"Christ! When was that?"

"Oh, about four years ago. I kept it quiet. Can you see me bringing up a kid, Maria? I'm just hanging on by my fingernails."

Although I'm not a creative woman, I can recognise the signs in

Beatrice from the creatively gifted people I've met. She has that omnivorous attitude to experience, the taking of great personal risks – without as yet any sign of the talent to put it to good use. This may be her tragedy.

We make our way to The Cricketers for lunch. We sit outside as we eat, gazing at the pond in the beer garden, thick heavy green in the shade, ducks trailing through the water.

"You know," says Beatrice. "Do you remember that time when we were girls, Maria? We paddled in that river when we were on holiday?"

"Yes I do. I'll never forget that."

"I'm just reminded of it now. It wasn't very far away from here, if I remember rightly." She turns to me and smiles. Her glasses magnify her eyes, deep and inscrutable as pools.

We were ten years old. "Last one in's an idiot!" says Beatrice and runs down the slope to the riverbank. The grass has a toehold in the mud before giving out to the lapping water. We tuck our skirts into our knickers, kick off our shoes and socks and step forward. The water shocks in its coldness; the mud is grainy on my toes. Beatrice is already further out, waving at me.

"Coward!" she yells. "Maria is a coward!" She chants it again and again, like a litany.

"I'll show you," I mutter under my breath and step forward.

At that moment it happens. Beatrice slips and falls forward with a big splash and goes under. I see her face, hair ballooning out around her head, darkening as she slowly sinks.

I start to scream.

The next thing I know, my father is running down the slope, diving in. I go back to the bank and sit there, sobbing in fear. My mother puts her arm about my shoulders.

Through blurry eyes I see my father surface with Beatrice in his arms, her dress hanging sodden from her, her hair a mass of wet dark copper. He lays her down on the grass, head on her side. Water drains out of her mouth. I watch as my father gives her the kiss of life, see her pale face, her lips already going blue.

"Come on, Beatrice, *breathe*," my father whispers. Then he looks up at my mother. "Kate, get some blankets from the car."

As my mother hurries up the slope I say: "Is she going to die, Daddy?"

He glares at me. "No, she is *not* going to die, you stupid child! Just shut up."

Beatrice makes a choking sound, then splutters up watery vomit, which spills onto the grass.

"There's a good girl. Get it all out."

My mother hurries down the slope with an armful of blankets. Quickly she undoes Beatrice's soaking clinging dress. I'll never forget the brief sight of her body, lying there, frail and cold in her underwear before my mother wraps her up in blankets. Beatrice's teeth chatter. My father lifts her up – so easily, she must be so light – and carries her up the slope. I rub my eyes, reddened from crying; my mother turns and offers me her hand. I blindly take it and let her lead me up the slope to the car.

Beatrice is put to bed as soon as we get back, and she will go down with pneumonia. My father smacks me and sends me to my room without dinner. "Don't you *ever* do that again! Beatrice could have drowned!" I lie face down on my bed in the dark, my tears soaking into the pillow. It's not the pain of being punished that really shakes me, even though that's unnerving enough: this is the first time he's done that to me since early childhood and rarely then as I was seldom naughty. It'll prove to be the last time. It's more the unfairness: I have after all done nothing.

"Maria?"

My mother's voice. A blade of yellow hallway light cutting through the darkness. "Maria, can I speak to you?"

She turns on the light. I look up at her, dazzled.

"You've been crying."

She sits down on the bed next to me. Still unsighted by the light, all I can see is her silhouette, smell her perfume. I embrace her suddenly, by blind animal instinct.

"Daddy didn't mean to hurt you," she says. "He did it because he loves you. After all, your sister could have drowned . . ."

Now of course, especially as I am a parent myself, I see things her way. It was fear that caused my father to lash out at me, for really the only time in my life. Before and after this incident, I was the paragon of his twin daughters, invoked *ad nauseam* when Beatrice defied or disappointed him. I am worried for James who is after all only six. But there are dangers in letting fear rule you. If I'm too restrictive towards him ten years or so from now, will he repay me with defiance, as Beatrice did to our father? So many mistakes I can make, with a human life at stake.

As we sit eating our lunch in the pub beer garden, Beatrice says: "I remember falling in. I didn't even feel the cold. It was like a sensory-deprivation tank: I couldn't see or hear anything. It felt so peaceful. I didn't mind it at all."

"Weren't you scared?" I say. "After all, you nearly drowned."

She shakes her head and lights another cigarette. "No, not at all. I knew someone would catch me."

Night-time. James has been put to bed and Beatrice and I sit side by side by the fire. Tiny orange flecks leap up from the coals, and smoke billows up the chimney. There's a cordiality between us that we haven't had for years, if ever.

I say, at the risk of shattering this calm: "Why did you do it?"

She pauses before she answers, her skin glowing orange from the heat. So long that I think she hasn't heard.

"Beatrice . . .?"

"Yes, I heard you. That was really – you could really say that was the latest of my pathetic little bids for attention. A cry for help."

"How can you say that? You could've died."

She smiles. "Like as in that river. I knew someone would catch me."

"Why did you do it?"

She shrugs. "I don't remember clearly. It was just a lot of different things. I'd split up with Nick a few days before – that's one. I realised how desperate my situation was, financially – two. And I had that sense – you know, I'm thirty now, and what have I done? Can I continue to live this way? Three. I felt I was drowning, and I wanted someone to catch me. I just decided there and then to do it. Spur of the moment." She leans forward and takes hold of my hand. "You remember that day at the river, Maria? I just wanted Dad to be concerned for me for once. I didn't do it deliberately, but it could have been subconscious."

"I don't understand."

"Well, you were his favourite. You can't deny that. I was forever being told to be more like you."

I nod. "It's not as simple as that, Beatrice. I do love you, but I wouldn't want you to be like me."

"But you've got everything going for you, Maria. You always did have."

I shake my head. "I do not. You always risked things. I've played safe all my life."

"It doesn't seem that way. I just seem to get hurt. I put my all into an affair and it goes bad. I probably just attract shits, men as fucked-up as me."

"But at least you *try* things. It's nothing ventured, nothing gained otherwise. Let me tell you something, Beatrice. I've never said this to anyone before. The reason Mark left me was because he was bored with me."

"*Bored* with you? How come?"

"Bored with me. Just that. He said I was cold, I didn't give anything to him. And he was right, up to a point. Please don't put me on a pedestal, Beatrice. I *am* cold. I don't give because I don't risk anything." This takes an effort to say; as I do so, I feel a sting in my eyes and a tightness in my throat, the prelude to tears. I look down at my lap and glance back up at her. She watches me intently. I whisper: "It's not you who's fucked-up, Beatrice. It's me."

There's a pause, and Beatrice takes hold of my hands. The fire splutters, begins to die. Then Beatrice says: "Shall we go to bed?"

I gaze down at my hands and say nothing, exhausted.

"I feel very raw," she continues. "I don't want to sleep alone." Another pause, then she says: "Can I sleep with you, Maria?"

I nod.

"Can I? Just for tonight. It'd mean a lot to me. We haven't done that since we were girls." And she kisses me.

Blue, deep blue, my sister's eyes. The windows of the soul. They show their history of hurt, of pain, of instinctual reaching out for something she can't name. Our orbits have diverged over the years, and I feel the ache of the string stretched tight to snapping point as the stone whirls round at its apogee. Now, at thirty years old, the midpoint of our lives, we are revisiting a time when we didn't have these hurts. And starting again.

That's How It's Been

BY DAVID NUTT

I couldn't even remember whether it was two nights or three nights when I couldn't say if I'd slept or not, dreaming and undreaming with some noise like a dog yapping or maybe a barn owl shrieking making me wide-clear and things all gone queerly sharp and kind of trembly. Going to bed quick after Mum gave me the cocoa and not wanting biscuits or anything and really not wanting to go to bed either, but anywhere rather than stay down, with Mum and Dad looking miserable-ill and Granny still spitting in the fire even though Billy's gone away – Granny still chammin' her lips and not doing anything but sit and cough, spit and say, "Wassatime now then?" or sometimes "I'm all right, don'ee fuss over I." And all the time in my mind no matter what else is going on or what I'm saying I keep seeing the man in the bowler and the policemen, two of them standing behind him, Mum answering the door and Dad coming behind her and me very nosey peering in between. Before anyone says anything Dad makes a sort of groan worse'n I've ever heard and speaks first in temper 'though I couldn't tell why: "What in the name of Christ 'as 'e bin up to now?" and Mum says "shush – mind the child." Her face is white like when she fell off the steps one day and hurt her head.

Dad pulled me back out the way, but there's only two rooms downstairs and he didn't quite shut the door, so I stayed close to the edge and I heard plenty, but couldn't make out why they should get so excited with Dad cursing and Mum shushing and the bowler-hat-man talking away. And I missed a lot 'cause Granny started coughing good and strong and there wasn't any pot with carbolic in it so she kept spitting in the fire and the draught of her and the door puffed the smoke out so she'd start all over again. I heard the man say "search warrant" and "he's gone too far this time, I'm afraid," so I reckoned that Billy was going to run away again, longer than before, perhaps even to Scotland or across to France, 'though why he should I couldn't see 'cause he idn't going to school at

Miss Bourne's at Bodmin now, he's got a job at the village, part time, with helping Dad in between when our crops got to be pulled or our two fields furrowed. "Come in then, all three on ee 'an search as much as you like 'cause 'e idn't 'ere, an' most likely what youm saying is true, as 'is own granny says that's 'ow it'll all end up."

Mum says "shush, mind, the child'll 'ear you." Though why she kept saying child instead of Winny I don't know.

It idn't the same anymore somehow, not 'cause Billy's gone a long way this time and they won't find him, but more 'cause of Mum staying white and dreamy sort of and Dad not saying much at all only staring, even when Granny coughs or wants to drink or something.

I go to bed in the same room in the same small bed opposite Billy's. It's all different too 'cause Mum never bothers to pull the screen across and I can see Billy's bed all the time, made up ready. But I can't go to sleep thinking of the bowler-hat-man and one of the policemen coming into our cottage and looking all round, in Dad's shed where he makes things, even in the barn and the chicken-runs.

I knew they wouldn't find Billy. Just as if *I* wouldn't know where he was! On that night, even before Mum started saying "He's late again. I suppose it's all right," I'd had his signal from the house on the hill. Two short flashes and three long. So I'd given him my O.K., three shorts repeated several times, and I knew what I had to do 'cause I'd promised to do it even though it was his secret what for. It was like a game we used to play.

Mum and Dad were arguing a long time before I heard them put Granny on the commode, her coughing and muttering, Mum saying "Shush, the child's got ears" to Dad and so I knew he was still on about Billy running off. Then when Mum came in quietly and leaned over me I was faking snoring, with my heart beating fast into the mattress like a drum-thump, feeling her kissing my ear, clumsy, and her face was wet. Suddenly I wanted to jump up and shout, "Mum, he's out there, it's all right," but a promise is as good from a girl as a boy – better I think and I'm nine now and Billy all the time kept his promises to me, all of them – so I waited and waited – once thinking I heard Dad saying "Shush, the child'll 'ear ee," instead of Mum saying it.

When it was very quiet I did what Billy wanted, with my jeans and sweater on, taking his wallet with money and all sorts of things in it along with that book of London and some addresses; taking it from under his mattress, stuffing it down my jeans, then climbing out the window with my daps on, down the ivy loops and stick-out drainpipe.

Half-way to the old house I was frightened 'cause I thought I heard voices and something made me think of the bowler-hat-man, and he seemed worse than the spooky stories Billy used to tell me in bed about vampires. If Billy wants to go to London or even America that man idn't going to stop him, I thought. I crept on and got in through the back window like when I used to be Calamity Jane, only I had his wallet instead of a gun with caps in. But when Billy came out of the half-dark I was scared more than ever because his face was whiter'n ever Mum's was and there was blood or the likes of it on his shirt. I could see a gun on the old table where we use to play at rustlers' hide-out and it wasn't Billy's airgun for the magpies but like my cap-gun only somehow it was for real, and Billy grabbed my shoulders and said:

"Good. Good kid. I knew you'd come. Where's the wallet?"

And I couldn't speak a word 'cause he was hurting me with his fingers biting in and he never had ever hurt me before. I couldn't understand why he hurt me or why his voice was different and his eyes too, all sort of red and wild, and inside I was crying – all inside shaking and crying and I wouldn't let it out because he hadn't seen me crying since I was six or seven and I knew it would spoil it somehow for him then and he said:

"Tell I then, 'ave you got the wallet, 'ave you got it?" Shaking me in little hard jerks, so I nodded and nodded 'cause of the crying trying to come out, and he let go so I was able to give him the wallet.

Billy looked inside and pulled out a big folded sort of ticket and grinned and put it back, stuffing the wallet into his shirt, and it was like somebody else grinning but Billy, so suddenly I wanted to go, the inside of me was all pain; I felt like bursting.

I started for the window and he grabbed me again.

"You go back quietly now," he said. "Promise me youm tellin' nobody about all this, promise?"

So I nodded till my neck ached and he let me go again and just before I went out he said "Winno" like he always used to and came towards me and touched my nose with his hand and said "Thanks Winno, youm a – a – damn it – hurry back quiet now an' don'y let a body see a bit on ee," and his voice was Billy's all right again. That was even worse so that I nearly fell down and when I got away from the house I ran and ran hard so the crying could all come out like steam and air rushing out not like crying at all.

The bowler-hat-man and a policeman stopped me, suddenly, along the lane where the badgers' holes are, and it was dark, but I knew it was him even though I'd ran into his belly like a ball against a wall only I didn't bounce 'cause his hand came round the back of my neck, holding me hard into his coat-buttons.

"Ah! It's Al Capone's little sister," he said. "Where is he?"

I was still panting, gasping.

"He's up there at that derelict house, idn't he?" the policeman said, and I could see he was our village bobby from Dobwalls. I shook my head like mad. "No, no he idn't there now. He went away a long time ago."

I could see their black car nearly in the ditch. They stared at each other.

"He's running away to America and you'll never catch him, never," I howled at last.

"There now, childer, there now," our bobby said, patting my head. "But what you bin adoin' up there a' night anyways?"

"I was playing hunters and animals and I – I – I wanted to trap a stoat."

Then I thought of our secret and promise and Dad asleep in bed, when they stared in a funny way at each other. "Please, please, Mister, don't tell my Dad and Mum, please don't tell," I said.

"We won't tell anybody about seeing you, young miss," bowler-hat-man said, with a queer little smile. His face was like a big brown pudding with two black currants in it. "We promise we won't tell a soul. But you hurry back to bed like you've done before, eh? You go back quietly." I thought of Billy 'cause that was just what he had said.

"He's not up there. He ran away to America, yesterday," I said. "Miles and miles away. You'll never get him back."

He let me go and patted my bottom.

"Yes, yes, we know. Now you run along, little girl, and don't be naughty again."

"You won't tell?"

"No, we won't tell, we promise."

But when I went on my legs seemed weaker and I kept stopping and looking back wondering what it was all about wishing Billy hadn't been like he was and that he'd told me all about everything even the big ticket.

When I was back in bed listening hard I heard some bangs somewhere outside and something sounding like a fox barking so I thought it was them in their big car and it backfiring when they drove it from the hedge.

Then a bit later someone knocked on the front door and I heard the bed creaking and Dad grumbling and Mum saying something in a funny sort of high voice but when I looked out of the window I couldn't see anything. It's that rotten big fat bugger in the bowler-hat, I thought, and now he's telling Dad and I shall get a smacking, and he said he wouldn't tell. But nothing happened only voices going on all the time. Then the noises were outside, footsteps and talking low, and I looked out and saw Dad walking away with the policeman and I couldn't tell why he hadn't come up and whacked me.

Mum came in quietly.

"Get back to bed, Win," she said, in a strange low voice, so I knew it couldn't have been about me the bowler-hat-man came.

"Why's Billy run away again?" I asked. "He idn't at school now, to run off and play truant."

"If he wants to go away he can and they won't catch him. So don't you worry sick, Mum. He's got a ticket, I know."

"Get back to bed," she whispered, and somehow *she* scared me too, and I wondered why everybody was changing and scaring me. I went to bed quickly, hoping she would kiss me good-night, but she just stood there near the door, staring, and I said "Mum" twice, yet she moved slowly, stopping to stare at Billy's bed before she reached mine. She didn't kiss me at all or even say goodnight. She sat on my bed near the pillow and when I sat up and said "Mum, where's Dad going with the man?" she put her arms round me and held me so tight it hurt, not saying anything only hugging me with her breath blowing into my hair. Her arms felt thin and hard and strong, but they trembled – all the time, until I heard a car or a van pull up and voices again, scuffling, scraping noises. "What's it, Mum?"

But she only said "Shush" and loosened her arms a bit. We stayed for a long time.

There were all sorts of noises, inside and out, and then Dad came in and he was white-sick too now, a kind of yellowy colour.

He stared at Mum as though I wasn't there and said: "In the kitchen, on the sofa, cleaned and tidied up good'n proper," in a soft voice I'd never heard before.

"No," Mum said. "No, I tell you. In your hut, in your hut on the big bench."

Dad looked sheepish. "It 'ouldn't be right."

But Mum was angry. I could feel her shaking inside. "No, no, not in the house, for God's sake."

"All right, don't get het up so, youm goin' a be sick worried. She'll have to know some day. She's old enough."

"After, after it's all over," Mum said wearily. "It'd be too much, too much."

He shrugged and went out.

"What's it all about, Mum? Where's he going and why does everybody look sick?" I asked, coaxingly.

"Never you mind," she muttered into my hair. "Never you mind. It's something bad we all ate. It's nothing. You just shush now," and we still stayed there listening to lots of scuffling and scraping, voices sort of whispering hard at each other, and once I heard Granny grunting and chammin, but nobody went in to her.

I keep thinking too of the daytime after when I looked at Dad's hut and all the windows had sacks over the insides and the door was padlocked, but I looked in through a knot-hole, where once a tom-tit got in and couldn't get out and I could see something covered up with a sheet on Dad's bench and I reckoned I knew what that was so I ran in and told Mum when she was washing the breakfast crocks.

"Mum," I said, "I know what's in Dad's hut and I guessed right away when I looked through the knot-hole, so that was clever, eh? But it'll be just as good though it idn't a surprise. Dad won't mind if I know, will he? Can I have a sixpence like when I guessed what Dad bought for Billy's birthday?"

She turned sudden and a plate fell out of her hands and she didn't seem to notice it only staring at me as though I was a bomb ticking or an adder or something, all frightened like, and she stepped on the pieces of plate, so I thought she might smack me because of it and her face was twitching, but she only said, "Winny, Winny, Winny," in a kind of wail which gave me a pain in the chest for sure like when a cow mooed over the fence one night in the dark and I didn't know it was there.

"I'm sorry, I'm sorry you broke the plate, Mum. I am sorry really," I managed to cry out. All she said was, "Tell me, what was it then?" So I tried to laugh but couldn't and I told her quick so she would forget about the plate and how everybody was sick from eating something and everything was queer and sort of miserable all the time now.

"It's a pig for a barb – barb – barbecue, and Dad covered it with a damp sheet like last time, I guessed last time too so he locked the door and covered the windows, but I peeped in the hole and could just make it out." And even when I was still saying it she gave a horrible laugh which idn't the sort people do when it's funny. I wondered what I'd said that was so bad 'cause she rushed out then across the yard calling for Dad who was sawing logs.

But when she came back she only threw away the bits of china and went on washing up so I wiped for her and I was afraid to say anything and kept on looking up at her to try for her to look at me but she wouldn't.

The next day I couldn't see through the hole 'cause it was blocked and they sent me to stay with Auntie Bess in the next coomb at Warleggan, 'cause they said they had to go somewhere where they couldn't take me. It was two days I was there and when I came it was all right in Dad's shed and the pig was gone and I'd never seen Dad's hut look so clean and tidy or smell sort of spicy so I knew they'd had the barbecue without me and I started crying 'cause it was mean and I didn't know why they made me stay at Auntie Bess's. And what with all those days before when Billy ran away and the bowler-hat-man was there and Mum and Dad so queer and miserable I wished I was with Billy in America or whatever anyplace, with like he used to be calling me Winno and all that and giving me pick-a-backs round the yard, so I didn't want to speak at all to anybody if everything I said was naughty and they were still sick from eating something maybe the pig now and still looking miserable and starey like.

I didn't speak much for a long long time, only when I was at the table asking for bread or something, anyway nobody was talking much and Granny was hardly chammin' or coughing any more but sort of tired and nodding all the time in her chair.

But this tea-time I wondered if they'd had a letter from Billy 'cause it was a long time and he was where he wanted to be, I guessed, and safe from the bowler-hat-man, so I said as grown-up as real when it was quiet and Mum and Dad was sipping their tea: "I wish I was with Billy 'cause it idn't fun here any more and I'll even be glad when you send me back to school and what're you keeping me home from school for 'cause I idn't sick like you and I might even run away like Billy when he sends a letter and I know where to go."

Mum put her cup down crash and the tea slopped over and Dad was tipping his and staring and Mum cried out in a terrible voice:

"Oh, my God, my God," and put her arms on the table in amongst all the things and her head sort of flopped down on her arms and her hair was wriggled on the bread and in the tea and she started crying, crying, crying.

It was terrible crying like her throat groaned when she breathed in and howled out loud, howled and groaned, so I was frightened more than ever or ever could be what I had said or done and didn't know what, didn't know anything anymore.

I ran upstairs quick, falling upstairs so quick and into the bedroom and on the bed with the cover'n blanket screwed up tight by my ears so's I couldn't hear Mum's terrible crying, but I could, I could, I could still hear her crying and didn't know why, and Dad's voice saying "There now, there now," some time when it was stopped and things were queerly sharp and trembly again, Dad's voice sort of deep and muffled through the ceiling saying, "You'd best tell her now. Youm bound to tell her."

So that's how it's been in our house for I don't know how many days and it idn't fun any more and this now was worse'n anything, even missing the barbecue and Billy running away for keeps.

I'd best lay here quiet now and just listen and wait for Mum to come up and tell me like Dad said their secret.

But it's a long time and I'm still scared someway, I don't know why, scared more than ever.

It's Travel that Broadens the Mind

BY GLADYS HARVEY

There was this Hungarian countess on Victoria station.

How do I know she was a Hungarian Countess? Well I'm no fool. You think because I come from Cornwall, and I'm not sort of . . . what's the word . . . sophisticated . . . that's it . . . sophisticated . . . that I don't know a Hungarian Countess when I see one. Besides, she told me she was, and why would she tell me she was, if she wasn't? I tell you this much it impresses my friends when I come back from my travels and say things like . . . 'When I was talking to this Hungarian Countess on Victoria station . . .'

Well poor things, they haven't got much get up and go, so what chance have they got of talking to a double-barrelled name, much less a real live Countess . . . couldn't handle it anyway.

I don't suppose I would have travelled that much myself if I didn't have to attend to a little bit of family business now and again, that's how I came to be on Victoria station, I was wondering if I could get to foreign parts with my Senior Citizens rail ticket.

Mind you, some of my friends scoff, jealous of course . . . can't . . . or won't believe me when I say 'Last week I was drinking champagne on Victoria station'. But it was true. It was like this, I was in the buffet on the Victoria station, eating what they have the nerve to call a Cornish pasty when this very posh lady came in and sat down opposite me. Well I could see she had class by her fur coat, and the way she shuddered when she looked at her coffee.

"I couldn't possibly drink thees feelthy stuff," she said, bringing a bottle and two paper cups out of a carrier bag. Then she said, "Thees you must share with me, I insist."

Well I said that I couldn't . . . possibly, on account of two sherries at Christmas had me swinging from the chandeliers so to speak.

She said nonsense, and that she couldn't possibly drink a whole bottle of champagne by herself.

Champagne . . . well I could hardly believe it, I had never tasted champagne, and here she was treating it like it was mineral water, well I said she had class didn't I. I said I thought it would be a bit embarrassing opening a bottle of champagne right there. Well I'd seen champagne bottles being opened (on the telly, and it looked very complicated to me, with snooty waiters with serviettes over their arms making a big deal of it, and as for car racing, the winners never seemed to get the hang of it at all, it sprays all over the place. I don't see how they ever get to drink a drop. Well it seems they do it differently in Hungary, her bottle had a screw top. Mind you I must say I don't like the taste of the stuff, rather have a drop of gin myself. Still I could hardly believe it, me on Victoria station, drinking champagne with a real live Countess. That in itself was worth the price of my Senior Citizens rail ticket, if I went straight home. Actually I did go straight home, took a taxi from Victoria to Paddington and home on the first train.

Well I had this new job didn't I. Sales Director of the Hungarian Essence of Youth. Actually you could have knocked me down with a feather when the Countess told me she was fifty three years of age, ten years younger than me, and didn't look a day over thirty five. It was all on account of this youth essence which she rubbed all over herself every day. Naturally I asked her where I could buy a bottle, and she said it was not in the shops yet. She explained that it was made from a secret recipe that had been handed down in her family from generation to generation. She said that naturally being aristocratic her family shrank from vulgar commercialisation but they had fallen on hard times they had decided to sell it discreetly here and there. "I approach the most likel . . . er . . . I mean the most intelligent looking person who looks as if they could do with it." she said. I must say I didn't care for that last bit, always reckoned I looked well for my age, and a whole lot better than some in the W.I.

But I didn't say anything, well poor soul, she wasn't used to hard times was she? Told me her fur coat was imitation mink from the Hungarian Oxfam, she wore it to keep up appearances, she had her pride after all. Besides I was keen to get this job for personal reasons. The little project I had been doing for years, which was a family business too, was coming to an end.

Still I thought I was on to a good thing here, after all my friends were into the anti wrinkle cream, Weight Watchers, and fighting the dentist tooth by tooth.

She said that, as I was obviously a keen go ahead type she would sell me as many bottles I wanted at five pounds each, although really she should be charging ten pounds. I took thirty bottles which was all the money I had. I had my return ticket of course, and she was very fair, gave me my taxi fare to Paddington, and enough for a cheese roll or something for the journey.

That's why I don't like my friends laughing so much, and what is more, not one of them will buy a bottle, not even when I offer to split one bottle between two. They say they are waiting to see what it will do for me.

Well it hasn't done anything for me has it, and I've got this rash. The doctor asked me what detergent I used, and if I had changed my brand of toilet soap lately as I was obviously allergic to something. I hope I'm not allergic to this lotion, not with twenty nine unopened bottles and no customers.

Besides I can't help thinking of the way the Countess put two fingers in her mouth and gave this kind of whistle and this fellow appeared with boxes of the bottles. I know I was quite tiddly at the time, but I thought I heard her say as they walked away I thought I heard her say "Bloody hell Bert, the effing Cornish aren't down from the trees yet, we'll work Paddington next week."

So I think it's just as well I paid them with Uncle Percy's money, and they didn't look at it too closely. Dab hand at the pound note was Uncle Percy, but then they switched to pound coins. He couldn't quite get the hang of the five pound note, it was good mind you, but not perfect, didn't feel so comfortable passing them on one of my little trips. Pity really because had Uncle Percy lived he would have got them perfect in the end. But he died sudden like, and I had to pay for his funeral with real money, and it's left me skint, and no Uncle Percy to fall back on. But I'll think of something, after all I'm not an effing Cornishwoman for nothing.

Morwenna

BY PATRICIA FRAZER

Morwenna steered the boat carefully around the bend of the Fowey river as John rowed. A flurry of gulls screamed up ahead of them and settled back to their endless, desperate search for food in the mud.

Morwenna had once startled her mother by saying the gulls reminded her of people; heads down all the time, scratching away at the land to make it yield the needs of living. Her mother said Morwenna was never cut out for the easy life if she had to start puzzling about everything she came across; and she'd better not let the vicar hear her say that. But Morwenna's mother had been despairing of her since she was five years old, and she never let the vicar hear her say anything except her creed and catechism if she could help it. Her mother had also said she'd never get a man friend with her head so full of nonsense . . . yet here she was, further from home than ever before with only John Tregenant for company.

"This is the furthest I've ever been from home, John," she offered shyly, still not quite sure how to make conversation with him.

"Never! I've been in Devon and Dorset, and once up to London. It's a fine world this – our Creator's handiwork. It seems to me it would be doing him a rudeness, not to try to see something of it."

"I've never thought of it that way, John. Not with the milking and the baking to be done, and the little'uns to look after – there's always been plenty to keep me busy handier home, without hankering to go up-country."

"That's blessed obedience, that is, Morwenna, but God wouldn't be so hard on you. You're a child of his, you've a right to be here."

"I can't get used to you talking about God as if he's a friend of yours, John."

"But he is. That's the whole point. Wait till you hear Mr. Wesley, then you'll understand."

Morwenna stared at a mallard family that was determinedly swimming after the boat; like Mr Wesley and his friends in hot chase after God. This was her first friendship with a young man; but in some ways it seemed hard that the name of the Almighty should crop up so often. She hadn't known quite what her friends talked about with their young men, but somehow she had never expected religion to be their main topic. Morwenna had been well grounded in her religious duties and her "I believes" in the creed were sincere enough, but John brought God out of the pew and almost carried him about with him, which seemed strange and not quite proper. Her sister had once asked if John had kissed her yet, and she replied she and John had other things on their minds besides kissing. But John was John, and if God came as part of the bundle; at least he was a bit more interesting in John's version than the vicar's.

They moored the boat as they neared Lostwithiel and John offered Morwenna his hand to scramble ashore. She wanted to keep hold of it; but knew what her mother would have to say if she was first seen in a strange town holding hands with her sweetheart, like any common creature.

She had expected Lostwithiel to be busy, being such a big town; but the streets were so thronged with people they could hardly walk; surely that couldn't be the normal state of even big towns, or people would never get their business done? The vicar had said John Wesley was a curiosity, like the man with the dancing dogs or the healer with bottles of coloured medicine; and people had nothing better to do than stare after any such. John was obviously more used to walking in towns than she was, she found herself running awkwardly at his heels, avoiding the outstretched elbows of several worthy citizens who wanted their fair share of room.

"It's a big place, Lostwithiel, John."

He gave a great bark of amusement and looked kindly down at her.

"The folk in London would call it the back end of nowhere, and say there was nothing to do here in a month of Sundays, child."

"They must be mad!"

"There's plenty would say they were, Morwenna. Run mad of the money-sickness, most of them."

"This Mr Wesley, is he a London gentleman, John?"

"He's from a place called Lincolnshire, but in a way he's from everywhere. He preaches to human souls wherever he can find them . . . he sometimes says the world's his parish."

"Must be lonely that, come wintertime. Who does he gather round the fireside and keep Christmas with, John? Mankind's a fair big family, I think I'd get lost among them all, myself."

John said nothing, he set his jaw determinedly and battled on through the crowd. There always was a determined loneliness about John, it was what had first made him stand out for her among other men. Everyone knew John Tregenant, but not as a drunkard or a bully or a comic-struck clown or any of the usual things men were known for . . . more as one who was one of life's fighters, prepared to spend his life battling with more than the soil or a fishing net. The gossiping girls said he and she were two queer cattle together; that nobody else would want either of them; with their speech above their station and their odd thoughts and dreams. But gossiping girls always said far more than was good for them or anyone else, their words ran like the little spring, pretty and sparkling and washed the stones clean, clean and empty as a whistle; like their pretty little minds. It didn't matter what others thought, said John, the important thing was to follow the light of what you thought yourself, while it gave you light to see by.

The crowd gave a sort of collective crowd-moo, breaking from every and no throat, and a man was carried on the crest of it, like kings of old must have been carried in triumphal procession, to either their glory or their shame. The man was of the usual manner of men, indeed, his riding clothes were worn and stained and his face bore the lines of tiredness, even illness. Yet he was very present; more so than anyone Morwenna had ever seen before.

"That's Mr. Wesley," whispered John, in the tones of one pointing out the eighth wonder of world. "What do you think of him?"

"Well, he's a greater man than Parson, or Trenhellian of Trenhellian's. He's even more of a man than my uncle Jez, when he's drunk and laying punches all about him."

"I'm sure being mentioned in the same breath as John Wesley is the nearest to glory your Uncle Jez has ever come, Morwenna!"

"I don't think he's ever looked to be close to glory."

Morwenna kept close to John and kept a tight grip on his sleeve as the great man began to speak. Her eyes kept wandering across the strangeness of that many-headed beast, a crowd. She kept being drawn back to particular people; a woman with a vivid shawl about her shoulders, a man with an ugly wen on his face. Yet all of them were family somewhere, loved and hated by someone. They just drifted across

Morwenna's life like a skein of flying geese, but to someone they were right up in the foreground; perhaps blocking out the sun. The preacher didn't shout, but his voice carried with no apparent effort across the crowd. Morwenna usually retreated into her own dreams in church, thinking of John when the vicar told her to think of her soul. But this man had words that stirred the spirit, words used in a way that fishing nets were used, in a way that caught men's souls. Morwenna was not sure what strange country she was in whilst he spoke, or for how long the talk lasted. She was even unaware that his closing words had come, and stood, still staring, as he climbed down from the box he had preached from in absence of a pulpit. People all around were crying loudly, like small children who had not learned to restrain their sobs. "I'm a sinner!" roared a hefty farmer in a tone which challenged anyone to disagree with him, "I'm a miserable, wretched sinner!" Shoving people roughly aside as if he were elbowing his way through a byre of cows, he suddenly caught Morwenna square in the stomach and sent her flying.

John pulled her to her feet and fought a way for them with his elbows himself, carving through the crowd angrily until they came to rest in a doorway where the press of humanity was thinner.

"Morwenna, dear maid, are you hurt?"

The tears were streaming down her cheeks; but she could not identify what emotion she felt.

"No, I don't think so."

One of her knees was almost certainly bleeding, but she could not look at her knees in a young man's presence.

"You don't . . . want to talk to Mr. Wesley?"

"Whatever for? It's just . . . so many people . . . and that man pushing me – if you don't mind, John, I want to go home."

"You shall, little maid. There's many folk shed a few tears at their first sight of Mr. Wesley."

They caught the tide almost at once for their trip home. Once in the cool and quiet, on the river, Morwenna was calmed again. Steering was a familiar duty, and the starlight lent romance to being with John. The fire of Mr. Wesley's words was still with her, as was the sting of the graze on her knee, but both were fading in the quiet sanity of evening. She inspected John's profile against what was left of the light. She had always laughed at girls who did nothing but dream of weddings – but perhaps married life would not be so tame a glory if it was with John.

"What did you think of today, dear heart?"

"I'm left with a shivering in my soul, John. Like the feeling when the storm clouds come up and the fishing fleet's out."

"There's something of the poet in you, Morwenna. Mr. John Wesley's brother, Mr. Charles, he's a poet. He can sing the love of God like no-one you ever knew."

"Is that his only song, John?"

"What others are there, child?"

Unexpectedly, John pulled for shore and anchored the boat.

"Dear one . . . don't be frightened, I mean nothing wrong . . . but I've something to say to you. I've not known you long, but . . . here child, you're shaking . . ." Helping her from the boat, he took her in his arms to steady her and all at once was kissing her, her eyes, her cheeks, her neck. So this is what it's like, thought the little piece of her mind that was disengaged from all this, so this is what they all giggle and whisper about. All this and Wesley too. Where will we live? she thought as she kissed him back. Will he give up his Wesley-this and Wesley-that, as we settle down to hard work and our own little'uns come?

"Morwenna, dear heart, you'll not think me too quick . . . I want to marry you, Morwenna. There. I've no gift of fine words, as I can buy no gift of fine lace for a sweetheart . . . but I want none of those gossiping young heifers, Morwenna. I need you, girl, you! Together we'll travel England . . . the world, perhaps, behind Mr. Wesley! Cornwall will lose us and it may count us well lost . . . but it's well lost for his parish . . . the whole world, Morwenna! All those hungry souls that need him . . . we'll have no cosy fireside, but the fire of the love of God to warm us. With Mr. Wesley's words and your words, and my willingness, lass, we'll . . . Morwenna, what's wrong?"

Morwenna had burst from him and was running blindly, crushing rank ramsons underfoot, into strange woods that were yet Cornish woods.

"I can't, John, I can't! The parish is world enough for me!!"

All her life, she was to remember her one trip to Lostwithiel and the stench of trampled ramsons.

At the Bottom of the Garden

BY LUCY SPEAR

Do you like gardening, constable? I was never much of a gardener myself. That was my husband Peter's obsession, the garden. After he died, I tried to keep it looking tidy, but I had no enthusiasm for it. I pruned the roses, and mowed the lawn now and again, and I used to wander up and down the little paths sometimes, thinking about Peter, and occasionally weeding around the flowers that struggled through.

But a large part of the garden was neglected and became rather overgrown. Peter's vegetable patch disappeared under a mass of weeds as soon as the warmer weather came. The tops of the fruit bushes stuck out like little islands above a sea of green. As the summer came, and the blackcurrants and raspberries ripened, the birds feasted on the fruit, and I left it for them.

There came a day in August, hot and cloudless, when I decided to shake myself out of my lethargy. It was not too late for a little spring-cleaning, I thought, and I took down the kitchen curtains and washed them. As I was pegging them on the line at the end of the garden, I noticed that the gooseberries were ripe. Now I have always loved gooseberries, and Peter grew one particularly delicious sweet variety, with a smooth reddish skin that would burst in your mouth to release the cool tartness of the juice.

It seemed silly to leave them for the birds, so I fetched a bowl from the kitchen and returned to the bottom of the garden.

I pushed through the weeds and crouched down to pick the berries. The sunshine flooded down on me, and the warm green smell of the garden surrounded me, and I felt happy for the first time in months.

The bowl was half-full, and I was about to start on the third bush, when I heard a noise; not a chuckle, not a squeak, but something between the two. It came from somewhere in the dense greenery at the base of the bush. I was curious to see what animal had made that noise, and I gently parted the weeds.

There under the gooseberry bush, hidden by ground elder and chickweed, was a baby.

I picked him up and held him in my arms, and he looked at me and smiled.

He was tiny, as small as a newborn baby, but his face wasn't newborn. He smiled at me with recognition and understanding, and his eyes – well, I've never seen a baby with eyes like that, nor any adult, come to that. They were a sort of golden colour, and you couldn't see any white at all. And the pupils weren't round, they were like a slit of black across each eye.

I knelt there cuddling him, and wondered what to do.

My first thought was to take him to the nearest hospital. He was quite naked, and I thought I should wrap him up in something, despite the heat of the day. There was something odd about him, something that wasn't quite right, apart from those disturbing eyes. I couldn't think what it was at first, but as I stood up to take him indoors, I suddenly realised what it was, and I nearly dropped him then.

You see, he had no navel.

There were other things about him that were different, too, I noticed afterwards, once I had decided to keep him. The tiny nails on his fingers and toes were pointed, like little claws, and under his shiny brown curls, his ears were pointed too. But it was the fact that he had no navel that made me decide not to take him to a hospital, not to tell anyone at all, but to keep him myself. I knew that he wasn't human. I knew that if I gave him up, he would become a scientific curiosity, something to be observed and discussed, perhaps even experimented on. I couldn't bear to think of him never having a proper home, never having somebody to love him, and I felt sorry for him.

So I kept him, and said nothing.

Because I knew he wasn't human, I didn't worry when he acted differently from human babies. He wouldn't drink milk, and I wondered what to feed him on at first, until I saw the way he looked at the bowl of gooseberries. I mashed some up and fed them to him on a spoon, and he loved that. He ate nothing but gooseberries for nearly a fortnight, and he was thriving. He grew plump and strong, and was sitting up by himself and beginning to crawl by the time the gooseberries in the garden were nearly all finished.

I always left him at home while I went out for my little bits of shopping down the road. I made sure I was never out for long, but now that he was so active, I worried about him hurting himself while I was out.

I hurried to the shops and back, and as I opened the front door, I could hear him crying in the kitchen, I found him sitting beside the open fridge, a lump of cheese on the floor beside him. He had bitten into it and spat the mouthful out again; he was clearly both hungry and frustrated.

As he opened his mouth to wail again, I could see that several little teeth had come through. They were very white, and they were pointed.

I picked him up and soothed him. Still holding him in one arm, I began to unpack my shopping basket. I put apples and carrots on the table, and then I reached into the basket and pulled out the plastic bag containing the lamb chop I had bought for my dinner.

He reached across and snatched it from my hand. Before I could do anything, he was tearing at the plastic with his hands and teeth, and had begun to chew the raw, damp meat with evident enjoyment. I sat him down on the floor and watched with some alarm as he ate the whole chop, worrying and chewing at the bone in the end, and contentedly licking the blood from his tiny hands to finish with.

From that day on he would only eat raw meat. At first I bought him more lamb chops, and a piece of steak now and then. But as the days went on and he began to toddle around, his appetite grew, and I had to buy him a leg of lamb, or a beef joint, every day. The butcher must have thought I was crazy, buying so much meat, but I didn't dare tell him about my boy.

I began to worry about what I could do if his appetite grew any bigger. I was eating little enough myself as it was, as it cost so much to feed him now.

Then one day I came home with some nice liver for him, and found him sitting on the floor surrounded by feathers. His mouth and hands were smeared with blood, and those unhuman eyes were glazed with satisfaction. The back door was open. I hadn't realised he was able to unlock it and go in and out as he chose. He had somehow managed to catch a bird, a blackbird I think it must have been. He had eaten everything except the feathers and part of the head.

The next morning, when I went downstairs into the kitchen, I found the remains of a cat. My boy had eaten all the flesh and left a ragged skin, the ginger and white fur all matted with blood. There were one or two clean white bones lying there, but he must have eaten the rest.

He lay curled up under the kitchen table, with his chubby hands under his cheek, looking like a sleeping cherub, apart from the brown smears of dried blood on his face and hands.

After that, I locked him in his room at night. This morning, I went to let him out, and found his room was empty. The window was open. I hadn't thought he could climb or jump from there, but he must have done.

He didn't come home until this evening. I had left the back door open, hoping. He toddled wearily over the doorstep and stood swaying slightly in the middle of the kitchen, blinking and smiling at me. He was radiantly happy, and he was covered with blood.

In one hand he held the end of a big stick which trailed on the floor behind him. Then I saw that it wasn't a stick at all, but a child's arm, gnawed off at the shoulder and partly eaten.

He's at home now. He's asleep under the kitchen table, still clutching that arm. I've locked the doors, but if he wakes up he knows how to get out. If you come quickly, constable, you should be able to catch him while he's still asleep.

I'm going to clear the weeds tomorrow. Then I'm going to dig up all the gooseberry bushes and burn them.

Bella Vista

BY ROY PHILLIPS

There was not much of a view from the windows of the Bella Vista residential home. By stepping into the large bay windows of the lounge and drawing aside the velvet curtains of the side sashes the guests could see the sea, across the promenade at the bottom of the wide tree-lined road in which the establishment was situated. Hardly any of them ever looked at it after a few days, so Mrs. Harris, the proprietress, had no qualms about retaining the name after buying the property twenty three years ago with the settlement from that swine of a husband who had left her for a beaded hippy and gone off searching for himself in the East.

Sometimes, Miss Tidmarsh drew the curtains aside, to determine the state of the tide or weather, before going for her afternoon walk. But even she never looked through the window for sake of the view. "Seen it once," Mr Ordish said, "seen it enough. I didn't come here for the view. I came for the food." He might have added that he also came in the hope that one day Mrs. Harris, after twenty three years of sexual abstinence would succumb to his ardour and bring up his morning tea herself, instead of sending that scrawny chit of a girl with the bony legs. Like many older men, Mr. Ordish was not yet dead, and he still had his desires. The thought that one so buxom in his bed might well see him off into paradise was a risk he would have taken gladly, and gone out in glory. Alas, it was always the girl, who, had he but known it, might well have done it with him because, before the Colonel came, Mr. Ordish was the most youthful and virile of the Bella Vista's twenty residents.

The youngest of the ladies was Milly Crabbe, Millicent, as she insisted on being called, who hadn't been here very long and kept herself to herself. She had made a distant friendship with Miss Tidmarsh, and occasionally went for a walk along the promenade with her on fine afternoons. She was a nervous little woman who might have been quite attractive in her youth had she been blessed with a more gregarious personality. Miss Tidmarsh was no fool; she knew what went on in the minds of women like Milly Crabbe, Oh yes, if Miss Tidmarsh was anything, she was conversant with human behaviour. She had read *The Naked Ape* and books on body language, and had been astounded at what she had learned about apparently shy and reticent people like Milly Crabbe. They had every good reason to keep themselves to themselves, for what they were trying to do, albeit subconsciously, was to keep themselves from themselves. And no wonder, in Gertrude Tidmarsh's view.

On the morning that the Colonel arrived, Gertrude was sitting in the lounge, reading a further treatise on human behaviour; well, one aspect of human behaviour, to be perfectly honest, but Gertrude had come to the realisation that she had been a lifelong Freudian without knowing it, and in furtherance of her studies considered it essential to keep abreast of progressive thinking. She always took great care of her books, and wrapped them in brown paper, stuck down with sellotape. She had made a habit of reading in the lounge in the mornings, for experience had shown her that it was at this time of day that the home was at its most active. Things happened at other times of the day, of course, but here in the lounge of the Bella Vista residential home it was from breakfast, at eight thirty, to lunch at one o'clock, with morning coffee in between, that Miss Tidmarsh had found the greatest scope for her powers of observation in the subject of human behaviour. The powers of observation in most people, Miss Tidmarsh believed, were sadly underdeveloped, but what with her studies, and her birdwatching, she had a trained eye and an instinct for detail. She would have made an invincible detective. Of course, Miss Tidmarsh kept these things to herself, as people less gifted might have considered her powers of observation as mere prying, but people were like that.

When the skinny girl brought her morning coffee, Miss Tidmarsh laid her book aside and picked up a glossy magazine that Mrs. Harris had left on the low table for the residents to read. Most of them were too poor, or too mean, to spend money on such trivia. Sitting in her vantage point behind the dusty plumes of pampas grass she turned the pages, glancing occasionally, with her shrewd, trained eye, at the comings and goings of the other residents.

There was Mr. Ordish, going over to sit with Mr. Thomas, where he would pretend to be absorbed in a game of chess while watching Mrs. Harris behind her desk in the reception area at the end of the lounge. He was a Dirty Old Man, Miss Tidmarsh knew, and Mr. Thomas a boring old, well, fart, actually, though she could never bring herself to even think such a thing. She turned the pages at discreet intervals, pausing at the pictures of country houses and flicking past the advertisements showing young women in brief and flimsy underwear. Some of them, she thought, even showed, but she would not wish to be seen looking at such things, the dark smudges of pubic hair through the diaphanous garments. Naked Apes, indeed! Gertrude wore respectable bloomers, as being symbolic of her chastity, and considered brassieres as disgusting sexist restrictions of the female body, allowing her own ample bosoms to sag and wander beneath her hand-knitted twin-sets as the Good Lord intended.

Here was Miss Crabbe! Such a restless little thing. Only been here three months, and already considering moving, going back to Torquay, of all places. There was absolutely nowhere to compare with Cornwall, in Gertrude's opinion. But Milly's restlessness was merely the manifestation of far deeper insecurity, there was no doubt of that, although one could never broach such a subject to one so close as Millicent Crabbe. Poor Dear. Those silly little chiffon scarves, with which she was for ever fiddling, were evidence enough of a life of frustrated coquetry. Probably wasn't allowed to flirt with the boys as a girl. These things were so obvious when one was trained in the matter. Gertrude came to the conclusion that she might even have made a better psychiatrist than a detective; they were much same, really. Millicent, indeed. If ever there was a Milly hidden behind a prim facade, it was here, behind those restless eyes which never seemed to look directly into her own. Gertrude would have bet on it, had she been of the type to indulge in gambling.

"Good Morning? Millicent. Come and sit down. How nice to see you."

Miss Crabbe sat down, and they discussed the possibility of Millicent moving on. "Oh no." she said. "Goodness Me, No. Nothing wrong. I'm very comfortable here, but I like to have a change of scenery, you know. And I'm sure you must all be getting tired of my chatter by now."

Silly woman has hardly opened her mouth, Gertrude thought. Keeping herself to herself. Afraid of some skeleton falling out of her built-in wardrobe, perhaps.

In her office behind the counter, with its plastic notice announcing 'Reception', Mrs. Harris gazed out between a dejected rubber-plant and a sun-starved tradescantia as she waited for the new arrival. She regarded her residents as retarded infants, and ran the establishment quietly, efficiently, and with a rod of velvet-coated iron. She could never understand why so many of them wished to spend their retirement years here in Cornwall. Most of them had left their friends behind, buried a spouse soon after coming, and spent their days sitting about the place waiting for the next meal, never seeing the sea, the harbour, or the beaches they had so looked forward to living beside for most of their working lives. It was tragic, but she had no time to be involved in tragedies, with twenty of them to look after. Her own tragedy, she had learned to live with. It was not so much the fact that the swine had left her in her prime, but the fact that she had allowed it to make her bitter. Her bitterness had, she appreciated now that it was too late, been only too apparent, and had repulsed any other men who may otherwise have found her attractive. She was now coming to the even more bitter awareness that much of the frustration of the past years had been of her own origination. At forty seven she was approaching the time when it would be too late to expect the attention of any men except for the likes of Charlie Ordish, and she feared, more than anything in her life, ending up like the people who came to her in their lonely old age. This place was now worth in excess of a quarter of a million, and she was a rich woman. It frightened her. It was too much, all of it, to bear alone.

Look at those two over there. Hated each other's guts, but were firm friends, nevertheless. This kind of love-hate relationship Mrs. Harris had learned to handle, along with all the other peculiarities of middle-aged, old, and lonely people. The new one coming today would present no problems. After a couple of days she would know his life history, as she knew the life history of all of them, for after a while the others became disillusioned with the newcomers and ceased to listen to them, regarding their own lives as of far more interest. It was to the staff, and particularly to Mrs. Harris, especially if they could be seen by the other residents to be receiving an inordinate amount of her attention, that they told their most intimate secrets. When she had heard it all, and found it difficult to concentrate on them any more, they either became silent or moved on. The men were usually the loneliest beneath their hearty, boisterous, or detached exteriors, as Mrs. Harris knew well, and she liked the men better than the women, as a rule, or rather, she disliked them less.

The new one, due to arrive at any minute, was a Mr. Hammond. That much, but not much else, she knew from the letter she had received from his sister, presumably, two weeks ago.

'. . . he has asked me to find a quiet residential hotel where he may be afforded the facilities of a private room for answering correspondence. After spending so long in the East he may be somewhat reserved, but you will find him of little trouble, and not at all fastidious in his requirements. I enclose sufficient for a three month stay, but he may well be a permanent resident if your establishment proves to his satisfaction, as I am sure it will, as you have been highly recommended. Yours faithfully . . .'

What was it? Alice Hammond? The signature was equally indistinct on the cheque, but it hadn't bounced.

They all said that, of course; may well be a permanent resident, and some of them were, or at least as permanent as old-age permitted. Mrs. Harris knew how to organise a funeral better than any of the local undertakers. She looked at her watch. Ten forty five was his E.T.A. as he had put it in his letter advising her of his arrival. It was that now.

Miss Tidmarsh looked over the top of her magazine as the hall porter struggled in with a large trunk. The hall porter was, as everyone knew full well, the somewhat grandiose title for the odd-job man, washer-up, second chef, and whatever else was needed about the place. Miss Tidmarsh had reason to believe that he was also something more than an eight hour a day employee to the manageress. She had seen him leaving very late at night, at times, and no blocked drain or light-fuse ever took *that* long to repair.

The trunk bore the legend, A.T. Hammond, Esq., for all to see, but Gertrude Tidmarsh, exercising her acute powers of observation, also saw, thinly painted over, the additional lettering, *Lt. Col.* A.T. Hammond, and what was it D.S.M.? She wasn't sure. But there were certainly letters, and letters, Gertrude was quite sure, gave a man, a person that is, status. The address was almost obscured, but the word INDIA was there as plain as a pikestaff. For those who used their eyes, that is.

"I wonder," Miss Crabbe twittered, fingering her chiffon, "what Mr. Hammond will be like."

Gertrude looked at her quickly from the corner of her eye with a glance of tolerant scorn, by far and away her favourite glance. She had several other glances, of course, like 'crushing irony' and 'amused indifference', but 'tolerant scorn' was reserved for those miserable wretches who struggled through life without ever exercising their God-given powers of observation.

"I feel sure," Gertrude said "that *The Colonel* will be a perfect gentleman."

She would be obliged to have a word with the poor man, or that Milly Crabbe would have her pinchy-paws into him before he knew what was happening. Shameless flirt! Lowered the whole tone of the hotel. Thank God she was soon to depart.

"Colonel? Gertrude." Millicent asked.

"Of course," Miss Tidmarsh said, off-handedly, placing the magazine on the coffee-table. "Didn't you know?"

The wretched girl came in to remove the coffee cups, and Miss Tidmarsh changed the subject. This habit one found in people of discussing people behind their backs was not what she was brought up to. "I am so sorry you will be leaving us," she said, "just as we were becoming such good friends."

"Well," said Millicent "I haven't made my mind up yet. It all depends." And she twittered softly, like a canary kept too long in a small cage, Gertrude thought. She knew the type.

He was nearly six feet tall, and all eyes were on him as he came through the main entrance, carrying a large suitcase without effort. So young, Miss Tidmarsh observed. And, though it was totally irrelevant, so handsome. Discreetly dressed, she noted, in lovat green, with a mustard waistcoat and soft-collared shirt. The tie, if Miss Tidmarsh was any judge, was hand woven. He wore highly polished brown brogues, and a gold ring third finger left hand, a widower, of course. His hair was greying at the temples. Gertrude's idea of the perfect man was a distinguished gentlemen greying at the temples. The image of the perfect man had changed over the years, progressing from a Corsican bandit during a teenage continental tour with her parents, but he had always managed to elude her. Not that she was ever a man-chaser, far from it, and in any case, there was still time.

Standing at the reception desk, he signed in, talking quietly to Mrs. Harris, his white teeth contrasting sharply with the tanned face and neat moustache. As he passed the ladies, on his way to the staircase, he smiled, and said "Good Morning" in a deep, modulated voice. Public school, Miss Tidmarsh observed with satisfaction.

She reached for another magazine. Of course it is vulgar to comment on other people in their absence, but, when conversing with the likes of Milly Crabbe one was obliged to drop to their level, so to speak. "Quite a gentleman," she said, casually.

Millicent fingered her scarf. Gertrude turned a page, proffered a quick smile to her friend. Millicent drew the hem of her skirt down over her thickly bestockinged knees. If ever Gertrude saw the manifestation of suppressed desire in the body language of a woman, she was seeing it now. "Do you know," Millicent said, "I think I've met him before." She returned her friend's smile with an apologetic titter.

That *woman*, Gertrude thought. She was the absolute *limit*.

"Well!" she gasped, and turned the pages with a ferocious determi nation, half expecting to see Milly's demi-nude photograph advertising some obscene undergarments.

Mrs. Harris tidied some papers on her desk as she watched the retreating figure of Mr. Hammond approach the stairs. He turned to take the first step and looked back at her. There was a slight, barely perceptible smile briefly on his mouth, and a knowing twinkle in his eye. She felt the blush on her cheeks, but returned the look. He may have seen the blush, but the other, more intimate flush was known only to her. She pressed her hips to the counter as she watched him mount the wide, thickly carpeted stairs. It had been a long time, she thought, too damned long.

Over the next few weeks he established a regular routine. Always the first down for breakfast, he ate at a table alone, reading the morning paper. Then he returned to his room, where he could be heard clacking away on a portable typewriter for a couple of hours, after which he came down again, picked up his mail and went for a stroll along the promenade to the post box by the quay.

Although the careful observer had occupied her hide behind the pampas grass, she had not been able to engage him in conversation. He had gone out, after raising his hat with a polite "Good morning", returned for lunch and spent the rest of the afternoon alone in his room. But, Miss Tidmarsh, quite by accident, happened to be over by the desk when the postman came one morning, and there was no doubt that the Colonel was receiving a considerable amount of mail. There were several official-looking letters in brown envelopes, and one or two redirected items had foreign stamps on them. Miss Tidmarsh was intrigued. It just so happened that the Colonel came down and Mrs. Harris appeared through the door that led to the kitchen behind reception.

"Good Morning, Colonel" said Miss Tidmarsh, smiling sweetly.

"Good Morning, Madam," he said, "Good Morning Mrs. Harris." He looked at Mrs. Harris, who smiled at him knowingly, but before she could speak Miss Tidmarsh said "Miss. Miss Tidmarsh. Gertrude Tidmarsh."

"Charmed to meet you, Miss Tidmarsh." Now, an untrained ear might well have missed the astonishment in his voice on hearing that Gertrude was still a Miss, but not Gertrude's ear; she was as adept at identifying birds by their call-notes as by their eye-stripes and wing-bars. "But it's just plain mister, you know. Plain Mister Hammond." The deep lines etched a handsome smile around his eyes as he spoke.

"Ho Ho," Gertrude said, "You can't fool me!" Dash it! Why did her voice always crack like that whenever she tried to sound conspiratorial.

"Ha Ha," said the Colonel. "Well, I must beg you to excuse me Miss Tidmarsh, but I have to catch the morning post." He bowed, very slightly, and turned to the proprietress, "Good day to you, Mrs. Harris." And that twinkle in his eye was seen only by her.

"Hm hm." Gertrude said as she watched him go through the door and pause on the step before striding briskly down to the road. "What a charming man."

"Yes," Mrs. Harris said. Charming indeed, she thought, but I hope there is a twinkle in more than his eye.

Gertrude retreated to her lair, and read the final chapter on human behaviour in her paper-covered book. All fascinating and highly informative material, she decided, and worth reading again. When Millicent appeared they exchanged the usual morning greetings and Millicent sat beside her dear friend.

"I had a word," Gertrude said, during a lull in the conversation, "with the Colonel this morning. Yes. Quite a chat, as a matter of fact. He is really a very charming man, when one gets to know him. Done a lot of travelling, you know." She pursed her lips, until the lines radiating from the mouth looked like the lava flow from a tiny, extinct volcano, and complacently ran her tongue around her teeth. "Been all over the world," she said.

Miss Crabbe smiled a mirthless smile, and fingered her scarf. "Has he?" she muttered. "Yes, most interesting, I'm sure."

Gertrude knew jealousy when she saw it. And she saw it now in the face of her friend, but things were come to a fine state if one could not have an innocent conversation with a gentleman friend and fellow resident without some people thinking the worst. She smiled at Millicent and turned her attention to the reception desk, and observed, with her usual alacrity, that things were apparently not running as smoothly in the administration of the Bella Vista residential home this morning. Mrs. Harris was evidently having words with the thin chamber maid. Despite the training of her visual faculties Miss Tidmarsh was, as yet, unable to lip-read.

Mrs. Harris led the girl back into the kitchen and into her office at the back, where all of the real work in running this establishment was done. She sat herself behind the desk while the dejected girl stood before her.

"I can not see," Mrs. Harris said, "why it should take progressively longer to clean the Colonel's room."

"It's very untidy, Mrs. Harris."

"That's what I mean. The place looks just the same when you come out as it does when you go in."

"He won't let me touch none of 'is papers an' that." The girl had omitted to mention when she applied for the job, that she had five 'O' and two 'A' levels knowing that she would have been turned down as over-qualified for a work experience scheme, but, so far, she had not forgotten to speak to everyone in the place with a broad Cornish accent and to act daft. "He's braem particlar." she said. "I'd do me best."

Mrs. Harris couldn't make her out. She was the best worker she had ever had, never had to be told anything twice, never answered back with insolent remarks, and actually seemed to enjoy attending to the needs of the old people, especially the men, whom a lot of her staff had regarded as lecherous old scoundrels not safe to be alone with. Yet, despite being so good, almost too good, at her job, she seemed so thick. Just listen to the way she spoke! She had to admit, there was really no reason for ticking her off. But she had been in the Colonel's room for over half an hour yesterday morning, three quarters of an hour today. She had still managed to complete all the other rooms before leaving work, but that was not the point. "Try to spend a bit more time on Mr. Ordish," she said.

"Mr. Ordish." the girl said.

"Yes. Mr. Ordish. You know who Mr. Ordish is."

"He doan like me in 'is room, don't ee knaw. 'e d' fancy 'ee Mrs. Harris." She went off into a fit of giggles.

Mrs. Harris ignored that, pretended she didn't understand the accent. "I can't think what you do in the Colonel's room for so long," she said, "try and speed it up a bit."

The giggles increased, and the girl's face became red. "All right," she said, "I'll see what I can do wid'n." and she turned to leave.

"Just a moment," Mrs. Harris said. But she changed her mind. It couldn't be. Not what she had briefly thought. With this bag of bones? No chance! "Oh, never mind," she said, repenting, "just try not to neglect the other residents. The Colonel is no different from any one else in this home."

Mr. Ordish was only sixty-two. He had taken early retirement and come here while still young enough to adapt to new surroundings. When he looked at himself in the bathroom mirror he didn't see an old body. In fact he was quite fit, and what deterioration there was had occurred since coming here. In summer he swam in the sea every day, and in winter, when most of the residents dozed away the afternoons in the lounge, he went down to the local gym for a workout with the weights before going for a long walk along the coast. Whereas he was now described as 'sprightly', in his youth he had been 'slight'. That was the trouble, he told himself, he was still a young man who'd had too many birthdays.

He played chess with Mr. Thomas with even less concentration these days. His mind wasn't on the game. Mr. Thomas thought that his friend was getting old, unless his own game was improving. What he didn't know was that Mr. Ordish had been letting him win for months. While Mr. Thomas deliberated for ages on the permutations of every move, Mr. Ordish directed his own concentration to the movements of Mrs. Harris's body as she brought flowers and vases of water to place about the lounge. She had recently taken to wearing tight jumpers and hip-clinging skirts, which showed off her contours far more effectively than those damned silly trouser suits women draped themselves in these days. He had been here two years, and not a single day had passed without him imagining the possible consequences should she come into his room in the mornings. He had taken to praying for it. Not praying, perhaps, more a sort of intimate conversation with whatever power controlled his destiny. 'Just one more sin, God, Old Man,' he said every night. 'Send her to my room tomorrow and give me something to repent. Make her randy for me and I'll send for the bloody Priest, I'll confess, I'll do penance, anything.' 'No chance', the power said.

It was the girl who came, and she took even longer now, shoving the blasted vacuum cleaner into every nook and cranny as if the room hadn't been touched for weeks. Funny girl!

"That your wife," she said one morning, "in the photo?"

"Yes."

"That you, standin' by her?"

"Yes." He took the framed picture from the dressing table and sat on his bed. Her loss had nearly killed him, but he had overcome his grief, and now, he hardly ever thought of her. Not now.

The girl sat on the bed beside him. He handed her the frame, smiling at her.

"Good lookin'" she said. "Got any more photos?"

He took a small album from his bedside cabinet and passed it to her. She turned the pages, slowly. Old wedding photos, some shots in a garden, seaside holidays – that one was taken here, before they built the concrete cubicles – Mr. and Mrs. Ordish at a party, – albino eyed and drunk. There was a recent one of himself emerging from the sea down by the prom. He looked lean and fit.

"Never look at them," he said. The girl was wearing an evasive perfume, something barely perceptible. "I'm not living in the past. Not yet." He wondered if she was anorexic. "You ought to be going to the Colonel's room," he said.

"I'm gone off he."

"Oh. Why's that?"

"Ohhh. You knaw." Mr. Ordish caught a quick flash of her grey eyes, and realised that he had never looked at her before. Not properly. She had long hair, drawn back into a coil at the back of her head.

"Like that, is he?"

"Bit" she shrugged, resignedly, as if these tribulations were the skivvy's lot.

With eyes like that? "Do you know," he said, "I've never asked your name." She only nodded. So he had to ask directly. It made him feel unaccountably shy.

"Morwenna." she said. "It's Cornish"

"Can you speak Cornish?"

"I've passed the examination of the Cornish Language Board." She blushed. She had given herself away. "Don't tell nobody, will 'ee?" she said, laughing. "You've got to be thick to get jobs down here. There was only this, or washing dishes, or working part-time in a supermarket for thirty five quid a week. I got thirty two on the dole."

He laughed, "You young devil." With her hair down, and wearing something other than this shapeless wrap-around overall she would be quite a different person, he saw. She was the type who would improve in looks and figure as she matured. Those grey eyes, when their depths were scrutinized, revealed a sensitivity already beyond her years. She gave him the album, which he returned to the drawer. How was it possible that this girl had come into his room nearly every day for the past six months and he had never seen her.

"You've made yourself invisible." he said.

"No I ab'm. You're damnee blind. 'cep for she with the big tits." Despite the mischief, deep in the grey, and her impudent smile, Mr. Ordish blushed.

The Colonel's typewriter was clacking painfully when Mrs. Harris approached his room. He could do with a secretary, he had so much correspondence. She tapped softly on the door.

"Come!" the Colonel bellowed. "Oh, I'm sorry Mrs. Harris. Quite forget myself. Old habits die hard, don't you know."

She was carrying a bunch of flowers. "I thought you might like the room brightened up a bit," she said, and began placing the stems, one at a time in a vase on his mantelshelf. "Do you like chrysanthemums?"

"Love 'em, Mrs. Harris."

She kept her back to him. Here goes, she thought. "Rosemary. We need not be formal in private, Colonel."

"Leonard," he said, from behind her back.

She placed the last stem in place. Turned to face him, smoothed her skirt and backed to the door. "I'll get some water," she said.

In the bathroom, she did a quick renovation job on her make-up while the jug was filling, and dragged her jumper down, tight beneath her skirt. Forty seven she might be, but she was far from past it.

"There we are," she said when the vase was filled, "nothing like the feminine touch, Colonel."

"Leonard," he said.

She went over and stood close behind his chair at the desk. "What are you doing? Writing a book?"

"Nothing as exciting as that, Rosemary, just answering letters, but my typing is dreadful." He pulled a sheet of paper from the machine and threw it aside. Put a clean sheet in its place. He typed the address at the top right hand corner. She leaned forward to examine his typing, and her breast touched his shoulder. His hand slid from her waist, over the curve of her backside, down her leg to the hem of her skirt. She drew herself away from him, went to the door, and locked it. "It's the girl's day off," she said. "We won't be disturbed."

To Miss Tidmarsh's annoyance, several of the lady residents at the Bella Vista had taken to spending an inordinate amount of time hanging around the lounge in the mornings. Once or twice she had found her favourite seat occupied. "They know darned well that I like to sit here," she muttered to herself. "It's disgusting. They were like a lot of . . . well, it only needed a red light over the reception desk!" She would have to leave, she decided. It was becoming impossible to live in such a sordid atmosphere.

As she happened to be near the desk when the Colonel came for his post, she had a few words with him, as usual, but he was evidently a very busy man, with little time for social intercourse. A little shy, too, she observed, but this was often the case with the masculine, outdoor types. When he had gone, she turned to Mrs. Harris.

"The Colonel is certainly a very busy man," she said, "I hear he is organising the Poppy Fund." This was true, but she had also heard that he was in charge of the War Graves Commission, and holidays for impoverished Officers (Retd).

"Well," Mrs. Harris said, "that's not quite it."

Private conquests are as hard to bear as public defeats, and she had the Colonel eating out of her hand. He said she drove him mad with lust for her, at a time when he had given up hope of ever finding love in his life. Quite touching, really.

"Actually," she said, ceding a little of her conquered territory. "The Colonel is an extremely kind, as well as a busy man. All the work he does is for charity." She leaned further over the counter in order to confide in Miss Tidmarsh, who was obliged to look away, the things people wore these days. Frightening! "You would be surprised," Rosemary Harris said, "if I told you he had sent a cheque for two hundred and fifty pounds to India only yesterday." She watched Miss Tidmarsh's face for effect. "*Two hundred and fifty pounds* for a new well in a little village in the hills."

"Really?" Gertrude had long since ceased to expect people like Mrs. Harris to know the difference between 'surprised' and 'astonished', so she let it pass. "How kind," she said. "As a matter of fact," Mrs Harris said, "I have been helping the Colonel with his correspondence."

"How very kind of *you*," she said, with a smile. So! There was no question about it now. Gertrude would leave with Millicent. This was no place for gentlewomen. Correspondence, indeed.

"I should imagine," Mrs. Harris said, "that he is quite famous, in his quiet way." She had ideas about a bungalow in the foothills of the Himalayas. Sell this place and go to India. "Yes," she said, "people send him money from all over the place. And he passes it on to where the need is greatest. He sent thousands to Ethiopia." There would be frangipani (or was it bouganvillea?) over the verandah as they sipped their sunshiners (was that what they called them?) as the shadows lengthened across the wadi. She pulled herself out of the daydream. "Of course," she said, briskly, "he doesn't want it spread around." She already regretted confiding in this silly woman. What business was it of hers. "You must excuse me, Miss Tidmarsh, I have rather a lot to do."

Miss Tidmarsh kept all this to herself. She watched from her lair with new respect for the Colonel. Once, he came over to her.

"Please forgive me, Dear Lady," he said. How charming and Old Fashioned he was. "But I am afraid I inadvertently picked up a letter of yours." And he actually sat beside her for several minutes.

"Oh, it's from that silly nephew of mine," she said, "probably asking for money." She was noticing, from the corner of her trained eye, that several of the ladies couldn't keep their own inquisitive glances from the direction of the pampas grass behind which she and the Colonel were enjoying their little tete-a-tete. Let them look!

Millicent Crabbe was among those who saw the two of them talking over in the corner, Gertrude noticed, and for some reason which was not hard to see, she kept herself apart from her friend for some days afterwards. Indeed she kept herself even more to herself, hardly ever being seen except when she scuttled through the lounge like a timid mouse, on the way to the promenade or the public gardens for her afternoon walk. How silly, Gertrude thought. There was absolutely nothing between the Colonel and herself. They were simply, good friends.

The Colonel had asked her to marry him. Rosemary Harris could hardly believe it. He was so handsome. And what a lover! She had asked him, to be honest, but he was too shy to broach the subject, so it amounted to the same thing. She had got him! He was going to take her to India, then the Sudan, where she would help him in his work. She was bursting to tell someone, but he advised discretion. "Don't want the residents talking," he said, "I'm a private sort of chap, Rosemary, m'dear."

She went to the estate agents in Fore Street. She wasn't far out, they said, Bella Vista was worth a quarter of a million – two hundred and fifty thousand pounds. They could sell it within three months. She was quite hard-headed with them, nobody's fool was Rosey Harris, after the struggle she'd had to build the place up. "What about your commission," she asked them, "and the solicitor's fees? Make it two hundred and sixty thou' to cover costs, leaving me a quarter of a million clear." "Can do," the man said. What with speculation on the government's intention regarding the care of the elderly, together with the local authority's reluctance to grant planning permission for any more old-people's homes, private nursing homes were at a premium in Cornwall. No problem, Mrs. Harris. "No boards," she said.

"No need to sell the place if you don't want to," Leonard said, "I've got a fair bit put aside, don't you know. You can let it." But she wanted to be clear of it all, not have the worry. "We'll be quite well off, between us," she said.

Would twenty do? Or should she make it thirty? With a determined flourish, Gertrude wrote the cheque for fifty pounds. It was her money, after all. A fine lot that nephew cared about her. The only time he ever wrote, it was to ask for something. All he was interested in was his filthy motor bike and that equally filthy, shameless thing he carried about on the back of it. Why should he have it all to waste? Far better, far far better, that the money should go to where it would be appreciated. When one realised that there were still villages in India without a well, to say nothing of the starving in Africa. She felt ashamed that she had not donated to such deserving causes in the past. There was so much good one could do in this world. Miss Tidmarsh would follow the example of the Colonel and become a philanthropist. She imagined all those dear little black faces queuing-up for water. The well might even bear the inscription 'This well was provided through the generosity of . . .'

At half past four she knocked on the Colonel's door. These things must be done in private.

"Why, it's Miss Tidmarsh," he said. "Do come in, Dear Lady. Please sit down. Rather untidy, I'm afraid." The poor man was as embarrassed as a maiden. How touching. "You know what we men are," he went on, moving a pile of papers from a chair. "There we are. Wasn't expecting visitors."

Gertrude sat on the edge of the chair, while the Colonel sat once more at his table. An Angel passed overhead, Gertrude noticed.

"Would you care for a glass of sherry?" the Colonel said, suddenly.

"Oh, well, hmm, well, yes, just a teeny glass, if I may, please."

He filled two glasses, and they sat sipping and talking until Gertrude quite forgot why she had come. It was not until she was leaving that she remembered to press the envelope into his hand.

"Now, Colonel, I have heard all about your wonderful work." She checked the Colonel's protest. "And I would like you to accept this little gift. Ah. No No!" She pushed his hand away and wagged a finger at him. "It's a small world, you know. You can't keep things to yourself indefinitely."

The Colonel was visibly impressed. "Well well," he said. "I don't know what to say." He was holding her hand.

"Good afternoon, Colonel," Gertrude said, retreating to the door, "and not a word to anyone about . . . you know what. Promise!"

"Promise." he said.

She was smiling radiantly when she left the room. The two old dears sharing room ten nodded significantly to each other as she passed them on the landing.

There was now a glint of shared conspiracy in the Colonel's eye when he met Miss Tidmarsh in the mornings. They were sharing a secret, and she felt the stirrings of long suppressed emotions when those eyes wrinkled into a smile. Once, she saw Miss Ryder from room fifteen press an envelope into the Colonel's hand, but she had not been up for sherry, Gertrude was sure of that. Nevertheless, she was not too happy about it. Mrs. Harris had said that the cheque he sent off for the well in India had been for two hundred and fifty. This induced some misgivings. She could see the inscription on the well as plain as daylight. It would be in granite. She knew a little man in Newlyn. In any case, she liked the Colonel's sherry, and he was almost an old friend. She would tell him tomorrow morning to expect her in the afternoon when that dreadful Harris woman had finished his typing, for she couldn't really invite him to her own room, not yet.

Now that Mrs. Harris had taken to cleaning the Colonel's room herself, Morwenna spent longer with Mr. Ordish. She called him Charley.

"That bloody Hammond." he said, one day when they were sitting on the bed together. "He's queered my pitch."

"With she with the tits?"

"Thought I had a chance before he came."

Her grey eyes looked at him, and he returned her look with a wistful smile. "Come here," she said, and drew him down, on to the bed, "what you need is a good cuddle."

Gertrude rose from her seat and joined Miss Crabbe, who was going for a stroll. "Thought I might join you, Millicent," she said "It's a lovely day."

They went along the prom, had a look at the boats in the harbour and finished up sitting on a seat in the public gardens. The leaves were just turning, and the autumn sun was warm.

"We might see the Colonel," said Gertrude, casually, watching Millicent from the corner of her ever-vigilant eye. There was no answer.

Millicent was being extremely quiet, even for her. The quiet ones were always the worst, as Gertrude knew full well. But as they watched the goldfish swimming in a tight shoal in the shallow water of their pool, Millicent said "Gertrude, you know we are not getting any younger."

I'm well aware of that! thought Gertrude. She was also aware that when people said 'we' in such a context, they usually meant 'You' are not getting any younger.

"No." she said, "We are not, are *we*."

Millicent pulled her gloves up her wrists, stretching the embroidered doggies beyond recognition as to breed, and almost to species. "I have something to say," she said. "But I don't know whether I ought." She was in a torment of indecision.

That was just the sort she was, Gertrude thought, tells you she's got something to say, and in the same breath tells you she can't say it. The people one had to put up with.

"Please, Millicent. We are friends," she murmured.

"Yes. Well, it's about Mr. Hammond."

"Oh?" said Gertrude, icily.

"I. You. Oh dear! Don't do anything silly, Gerty. I mean women like us can make such fools of themselves."

Gerty, indeed! "I can assure you, Miss Crabbe, that I am perfectly capable of living my own life, and when I need advice, I shall be glad to ask for it." She stood up in indignation. "And as for the Colonel, Well!" she laughed, a little, carefree laugh.

Miss Crabbe was desperate. "Oh Dear," she moaned, wrenching the gloves until the fingers were in danger of detachment.

"If you don't mind," Gertrude said, sitting down again, "I would rather the Colonel's name was omitted from our conversation in future". She glanced around the garden with amused indifference, this, she felt, being the most appropriate glance for the occasion. What was the

Colonel to her? Merely a very good friend. Make a fool of herself indeed! Dear dear. She was chuckling to herself most of the way back to Bella Vista.

It was a couple of weeks later that she was sitting by the pampas grass with a cheque in her handbag, waiting for the Colonel to come through the lounge, when two tall gentlemen came in an asked for Mrs. Harris. Were they from the estate agent, she wondered, for there had been rumours about the town that the place was up for sale. No. They looked like Guardsmen, in mufti, or should one say civvies these days. Must get it right, now that she was moving in military circles. One thing she noticed immediately. They were kindred spirits in their powers of observation. One stayed by the reception-desk, talking to Mrs. Harris when she appeared, while the other took a key and went up the wide stairs. Mrs. Harris, unless Gertrude Tidmarsh was very much mistaken, had tears in her eyes, but the gentleman was evidently reassuring her.

Turning the pages of her magazine she came upon the illustration of a country house, the sort of house the Colonel should live in. And no doubt would, were it not for his charity work.

Presently the Colonel came down with the tall gentlemen who had gone upstairs. What a handsome pair they made, Gertrude thought. The two strangers must be from the foreign office. One of them was quite dark, had Indian blood, perhaps, come to make arrangements for another well, possibly the one which her cheque would pay for. How exciting! The Colonel raised his hat as he passed, "Good Day, Gertrude," he said, "Good Morning, Rosemary."

The sound of her christian name from this handsome man was like a drug to Miss Tidmarsh, who watched with admiration as the Colonel, carrying a small valise, left the Bella Vista with a tall gentleman on either side of him.

Rosemary Harris suddenly burst into tears and rushed through the door to her private office at the back of the kitchen.

Outside, on the steps, the Colonel paused in the sunshine, and breathed deeply of the the salt-tanged air.

"How did you do it?" he asked.

"We didn't, to tell the truth, Arthur. You did it yourself, by changing your name again. Little Miss Crabbe recognised you from Torquay. If you were still Major Smythe, you could have touched her for another hundred quid."

"Pity." The Colonel smiled, a brief, wry smile. "But there is no law against changing one's name, you know. And I've certainly never called myself Major, or Colonel, or anything but 'mister.'" He smacked his lips thoughtfully.

"You chaps are wasting your time," he said. "I'll tell you what. None of that lot in there will go into court and give evidence, make Damned fools of themselves. Even if you've got one or two, Miss Crabbe for instance, I've given more than enough to various charities, thousands of pounds, to cover what I've received from them." He tapped his valise. "Kept the receipts, too."

"Besides," he said, cheerfully. "What's a man supposed to do when people keep shoving money into his hand, calling him 'Colonel' for no reason at all, and rich women propose marriage." He looked from one to the other of his tall companions. "She asked me you know! I didn't suggest it."

He straightened his back, and looked back at the Bella Vista. "Very comfortable place," he said. "Recommend it."

From the bedroom on the first floor Mr. Ordish and his young friend watched the trio departing down the road.

"She's going to need somebody now, Charley." Morwenna said.

A Requiem for Reynard

BY PEARL CARRINGTON

One cold February morning we were watching the Hunt meet. There had been a slight frost during the night. Not sufficient to harden the ground but enough to tighten up the mud by the roadside, enough to put a thin layer of ice on the duckpond, enough to make your toes tingle inside your 'Wellies' and the tip of your nose feel icy cold. "Not to worry" my Dad would say, tousling my long straight hair. "A cold nose means that you are healthy".

My Dad. He caressed my head in much the same way as he would our sheep dog, Prince. Sometimes when he returned from market of a Wednesday, I doubt if he could tell the difference. I noticed that he laughed a lot on Wednesdays, that his eyes were a bit more bloodshot than usual (even more than when he had been up all night with a cow calving) and he seemed to stagger a bit when he climbed down from the trap. Mam used to say that it was a good job Bess, our old mare, knew her own way home else the drunken old beggar would never have made it. Dad would laugh and show us how he could stand on one leg and drink a cup of tea without spilling a drop, which he said proved he was quite sober. Mam would shout at him to stop making a fool of himself in front of his only child, me . . . Poor Mam she need not have worried. I found it all very amusing and at least it made Wednesdays different from all the other days of the week.

The local hunt met on Thursday mornings at eleven o'clock, choosing a market square . . . or similar venue each week. On this particular occasion they met in the forecourt of the Black Swan Hotel. The small hotel was in the main street of our small Leicestershire village. No one knew why it had such a grand title, it was a public house really, but the landlady did let a room sometimes. The village school was on the opposite side of the road and the teacher had allowed all the pupils to go outside to watch.

I crawled through a hole in the hedge surrounding the school playground and joined my father who was standing pint pot in hand beside the pub door.

"Dad, can I have a sip?" I asked. He shook his head.

"This stuff is no good for little girls". The pot looked as if it was full of beer, but Dad assured me that it was just a hair off the dog . . . I had a strange feeling that he was in for another verbal battering from Mam.

Clutching his large warm hand tightly, I popped the thumb of my other hand into my mouth and sucking contentedly I regarded the proceedings through the narrow slit left between my fringe and my forefinger, which was hooked over the bridge of my nose.

There were gentlemen in bright red coats and ladies dressed in long black or grey gowns sitting side saddle and looking extremely haughty with their top hats tied on with black net. Grooms and servants were handing round drinks and snacks. The noise of children shrieking, hounds baying and the clattering of the horses hooves on the cobbles made me glad of the comforting nearness of my Dad.

"Dad," I murmured through my thumb, "Why do they hunt foxes?" I never heard his reply, because at that moment the school bell rang and I scurried back through the hedge.

The following afternoon when we were out at playtime we saw a great monster fly right over our school playground. I was terrified and hid under the hedge, but our teacher told us that it was nothing to be afraid of and that it was the Air-ship R.IOI. She was wrong though, because soon afterwards it killed a lot of people. I heard my Dad telling Mam that it had crashed in flames near a place called Paris. I remember she sniffed significantly and said that they were probably all drunk. A teetotaller all her life, she blamed the demon drink for everything that went wrong.

On Saturday morning I went for a walk with my friend Renee Gee. We pushed my doll's pram, Renee didn't have a pram but because we were friends, I let her doll sit in the pram with my doll and we took it in turns to push.

We wandered along the lanes to the woods in Wistow Park. At that time of year the woods were carpeted with snowdrops. They looked so beautiful and we decided to gather some and take them home for our mothers. We found a hole in the fence and crawled through. It was like being in heaven, Renee said, but I remembered the Pantomime I had been to at Christmas and thought that Aladdin must have felt like us when he discovered his magic cave. Do you remember how excited he was and then that awful Abanazer came along and spoilt it all. Well that is just how it was for Renee and me. We were so engrossed in picking the snowdrops that we failed to notice old Briggs the game-keeper from the Hall approaching on his bicycle.

"Hey . . . What do you little beggars think you are up to?" he bellowed as he dropped the bike into the ditch and came charging after us waving an enormous shot-gun in the air. The way he raved and carried on, anybody would have thought we were pinching the Crown Jewels instead of a few snowdrops.

Renee screamed in terror and promptly wet her knickers. I pushed my hand holding the precious posy up under my dolly's skirt and looked up at the red faced maniac towering above me.

"Hello, Mr Briggs" I said, trying to keep the fear from my voice. "I am sorry if we are doing wrong. We were only picking a few flowers for my Mam".

The old man's face softened when he recognised me. Briggs was quite friendly with my parents and often dropped in for a cup of tea and a piece of homemade shortbread. He calmed down a bit.

"You are trespassing" he said, "but apart from that, it is dangerous, there are traps set to catch poachers and you could be hurt very badly if you got caught in one o' they". We scrambled back on to the road. Poor Renee cried all the way home because her legs were chapped where she had wet them.

Many years passed before I again visited the woods in Wistow Park. I think my companion's name was Ralph. There were no snowdrops there then although I could have done with a bit of help from Mr. Briggs, when dear old Ralph started his hanky-panky and damn nearly deflowered me.

As the weeks passed and Spring turned to Summer, the days got longer and the evenings were warmer. Mam let me leave my windows open at night and I would lie and listen to the nocturnal sounds of the countryside. Owls hooting, sheep bleating, dogs howling and occasionally the sharp yap of a fox as he hunted for his supper. One night I actually heard a nightingale. I called my mother and together we sat on the low window seat in my bedroom and listened to his song. She held me close and I thought I would die of sheer happiness.

On May twenty-ninth it was my birthday. I was seven years old. It was a Wednesday and Dad went to market. Mam let me have a party and all the children in the village were invited. I suppose that sounds rather grand, but ours was a very small village.

My guests were very impressed with the pony Dad brought home for my birthday present, but even more so by his standing on one leg tea drinking trick. I recall that Mam was not so pleased and had to be restrained from pouring the remains of the trifle over his head.

That was the year that Dad decided there was money to be made in poultry. He bought timber and built a lot of chicken houses which he filled with hens. He also bought some cockerels and an incubator. He placed the eggs that the hens had laid into this magic machine which in a matter of three weeks turned them into lovely fluffy chicks. It was like Aladdin's cave all over again.

Abanazer, sorry, I mean Mr Briggs the gamekeeper, came along one day to borrow some of our broody hens to sit on his pheasants' eggs. He was quite friendly with me now, especially since my Dad was doing this big favour and he invited Renee and me to visit the Hall to see the baby pheasants.

"Why do you hatch them?" I asked curiously.

"So that his lordship can invite his friends to come along next winter and shoot them," was the reply. I pondered over this for several seconds.

"Why do you go to all the trouble to hatch them, if all you are going to do is kill them again?" I queried.

Summer drew to a close and the days grew much colder. Mam insisted on my window being kept closed.

"We haven't got money to warm the garden" she said. Sometimes there would be beautiful fern-like patterns all over the window panes when we pulled back the curtains in the morning.

"Jack Frost has been," Mam would say. "He makes those patterns with his fingers when he tries to get in for a warm".

In October the Hunt started coming round again. My Dad said they were cub hunting. It filled my heart with dismay to think of those delightful little animals I had watched rolling about in the meadow being chased by those enormous hounds. Dad seemed unperturbed by all this and I suspected he was secretly pleased, since we had lost a few hens recently and he was sure they had been taken by a fox. I had a few ideas of my own about the fate of our hapless poultry but I had no proof and it seemed pointless to tell him about the chicken bones I had seen in certain people's dust bins. Dad was never sure about how many head of stock he had anyway. It really depended how long he had stayed in the Black Swan, on how many he could see.

My riding had improved and I could almost go without the leading rein.

"You will soon be good enough to follow the hounds" Dad said. The hunt allowed the farmers to follow behind the members of the hunt. They did this I assumed to keep on good terms with them and so avoid any disputes over riding across their land.

Taffy, my pony loved the hunt. He would go wild with excitement when he heard the sound of the hunter's horn blasting the clear frosty air. There was no holding him, with one mighty leap he was over the gate and gone. Racing off to join in the chase. I would then spend the rest of the day searching for him, sometimes he would go for miles. Fortunately he was well known for this and our neighbours would often catch him for me.

On one occasion when this happened, I ran across the paddock trying to head him off and I saw the hunt in full cry heading towards our poultry houses. I was just in time to see a magnificent dog fox dive under the wire fence and take refuge in one of the chicken pens. The terrified hens flew in all directions as the hounds raced up to the wire howling and leaping in a futile effort to reach their prey who was crouching and snarling defiantly in a corner of the pen.

I watched fascinated as one of the red-coated gentlemen dismounted from his horse and wrenched up the wire fence with the handle of his riding crop, letting in the hounds who, in a matter of seconds, tore the wretched fox to pieces. I stood there holding on to the wire for support, the tears pouring down my cheeks, screaming abuse at the red-coated monster who was triumphantly holding aloft the tattered remains of what a few minutes before had been a proud and beautiful creature. At that moment my Dad arrived and gathering me up in his arms carried me home. I lay sobbing and bewildered in his arms.

"Why Daddy, why?"

"Hush baby," he said softly, "'Tis naught to worry your pretty head".

Several months later the postman delivered a large square parcel. It was addressed to me. It was unusual for a little girl to receive presents through the post, when it wasn't even her birthday. My fingers trembled with excitement as I struggled with the wrapping. I opened it eagerly. Inside was the head of the ill fated fox, mounted on a wooden shield. I threw up.

The years have passed by. I left the country when I married a city boy. Mam and Dad are both gone, the farm has new owners. I still have the fox. He hangs in my hall and has often been the subject of comment from my aquaintances and friends . . . Remarks like the paper boy made one day "I bet he was shifting when he came through that wall missus" or the woman selling flags for the R.S.P.C.A. "I cannot understand how anyone could have a thing like that in their house".

What does one say to these people? Over the years he has had a pipe stuck in his mouth, a bow tie put round his neck on the occasion of my daughter's wedding. Paper hats at Christmas and sundry other indignities which he has suffered with stoic silence . . . as indeed I have.

Sometimes when I am alone I think of those far off days spent on the farm and I remember my Dad saying that the death of the fox was "Naught to worry my pretty head". He was right of course, because we all must die. It was not the death of the animal that has haunted me all these years, it was the look of savage joy on the faces of the perpetrators.

Last Round

BY HARVEY KURZFIELD

The blow when it came was completely unexpected. He thought that he had the bout sewn up in this, the penultimate round. The old man's legs had begun to shake, he could hardly have been able to see through those puffed-up eyes; yet Denny had been warned by George, his trainer:

"Watch out for those haymakers of his . . . they've caught a lot of suckers."

But still he hadn't spotted it coming. One moment he had been filled with jubilation, knowing that his skill and youth had won him the match for sure; the next instant a rush of air startled him, his guard dropped, and his world suddenly exploded as for a brief, painful spasm he literally saw stars before his eyes. The roaring in his ears gathered strength as the vast crowd around the ring rose, crying out its distress or joy at this sudden change of fortune. The jeers at the champion's fumbling inefficiency to penetrate Denny's shield turned to cheers of renewed interest. The faces at the ringside had wide open mouths, like wolves awaiting a victim to fall prey to their scavenging teeth. Denny's eyes glazed over at the sight of those predators, then he seemed to be floating, all cares gone. "ONE!"

* * * *

". . .ce upon a time there were three bears . . . and they lived . . ."

"It's alright, Gran, you don't have to read me a story, I, I feel quite tired now already."

Denny performed an elaborate yawn for his gran's benefit.

"Oh, you're sure then, are you?" She seemed upset. He tried to soothe her distress:

"Yes, but thanks anyway, I really am tired . . . I'll soon fall asleep."

"Mm, well . . . alright then . . . I'll leave you to sleep."

She got up and hobbled across the room, stopping by the light switch.

"Do you want your light left on?"

"No, Gran, that's alright, I don't need it."

With the light switched off he grinned smugly to himself . . . Do I need the light; the three bears; cor, what's she think I am, a ruddy baby. I'm nearly eight, I can sleep in the dark . . .

When his gran reached the bottom of the stairs she switched off the landing light. Denny's room was no longer illuminated from outside – in fact, for an instant, everything was completely black. Denny sat up swiftly, his eyes suddenly filling with tears. "Oh, Gran!" he whimpered to himself. "You've turned out *all* the lights!"

He had never gone to bed with the lights off completely. There was no sound from below.

"— Oh muvver she's not even watchin' telly! She must've gone to sleep herself. Bloody fine baby sitter she is."

As his eyes grew accustomed to the darkness, Denny became aware of the large mahogany wardrobe against the far wall. His eyes opened wider and it seemed that as he watched, not only did the wardrobe begin to grow bigger but also the door began to open. He sat trembling, the blankets no longer warming him; then when he was sure that the door was really going to open and unnameable things were about to leap on him, he dived under the covers, pulling them over his head.

"Please don't let 'em get me, please . . . I'll let Granny read me a story next time, please, please."

He didn't know how long he remained under the blankets, but when he was certain there were no bogeymen about he began to relax and however hard he tried to remain awake his eyes gradually closed and he slept.

Then the landing light was on once more and his father's heavy footsteps were approaching.

"Hallo son, you still awake?"

Denny rubbed his eyes and looked up.

"Mm, what . . .?"

"Oh, just woken up 'ave you? Been sleepin' wiv no lights on at all, that's a boy."

Denny grinned at his dad's praise.

"D'you have a good time Dad?"

"Yeah – good picture. That Jane Fonda's not bad really – pretty good pair of knockers."

"What Dad?"

"Knockers! Don't you know what they are yet?"

His dad chuckled to himself and warm beery smells partially anaesthetised Denny.

"Knockers! You'll soon learn my son, you'll soon learn . . ."

* * * *

"TWO!"

— Only two? Two what? What . . .?

He couldn't feel a thing. He couldn't see anything.

— What happened? What's that buzzing noise? Why can't I move —? A movement of his head brought more pain directly behind his eyes and as the buzz outside his head gradually faded into the distance he thought he heard a voice.

"THREE!"

* * * *

"Three pounds Denny! Ooh I can't, you've only earnt four this weekend."

"No, go on Mum, I want you to have it."

"But won't you need some for tonight – I thought you were going out with that girl of yours?"

Denny smiled at the thought of Grace.

"She's all right. We go dutch – you know, she pays for herself."

His mother looked dubious and shook her fast-graying head.

"Hmm, in my day a girl liked to be treated, fussed over, brought flowers and chocolates . . ."

Denny grinned happily.

"Grace n't like that, she's quite happy as we are – besides she knows I've gotta help out in the house since well, Dad went . . ." He glanced at his mother, whose head had jerked at the mention of 'Dad'.

"Oh," he groped for words. "I'm sorry, Mum, I shouldn't have . . ."

"No, it's alright now Denny I've got used to the idea of not having him around; he's gorn his own way and left us to go ours. We're managing, we're managing."

She turned away quickly and Denny knew that in a moment she would go upstairs to hide her grief.

"You'll always have me around, Mum," he called after her. "Always."

— Well, nearly always, for a while yet —

Later he called round at his girl friend's house. He'd hardly finished ringing the bell when Grace hurriedly opened the door, pulled him in and kissed him vigorously on his surprised lips. Denny found himself blushing and was furious.

"Ooh, you look wicked with your eyebrows raised like that – you could do anything with me!"

"What the bloody 'ell's got into you?"

"How masterly you are – take me, take me."

"Blimey, Grace, your parents . . ."

"My parents are out Denny boy."

Grace smiled in what she hoped was a seductive fashion and began to unbutton her blouse . . .

* * * *

"FOUR!"

— Christ! I've got to get up, but I'm so tired: hot: wet. I'm wet! I'm soaked through. Jesus! Open your eyes – try – damn it – try —

Denny opened his eyes and let them widen with terror at the face glaring down at him; it seemed to be all teeth. Then the teeth were moving and something else . . . He's going to hit me, hit me —

"FIVE!"

* * * *

"Five minutes Denny that was a bit quick wasn't it?"

"I'm sorry, Grace . . . I . . . just got all excited . . . I couldn't stop myself."

He turned and looked down at Grace who lay quite naked and whose bottom lip pouted sulkily. His eyes ran over her figure, a figure which for a sixteen-year-old was more than amply proportioned.

"Gosh, Grace I never thought . . ."

"Never thought what? That I was sexy. Gawd, you make a girl feel wanted!"

Abruptly she turned her back towards him, then turned again to lie on her stomach. Her well-rounded bottom wobbled as she moved and dimples on either side seemed to wink at Denny. He began to blush again, but this time, instead of being furious, he found the experience pleasurable and carefully he began to stroke Grace's soft curving flesh. She looked at him with something like a gleam of triumph – she made no comment but slowly began to move her body closer to Denny.

Rather more than five minutes later they both lay, arms and legs casually entwined, their bodies relaxed. Denny closed his eyes and felt an overwhelming sense of comfort, luxury and confidence somewhere inside himself.

— Well Denny boy, he thought to himself,

— What do you make of this? Grace. What's happened? What is she? Whore, tart or bloody fairy godmother? Whatever she is she's done bloody wonders for me. Incredible. I've never really . . . you liar, 'cos you 'ave. You always fancied her. Just too scared to do anything about it. And now she's done it for you. God, if only Dad could see me now! —

Crossing the gap of time he could hear his father, chuckling once again:

"Knockers, son, you'll soon learn, you'll soon learn . . ."

And as the throaty, rich chuckles began to grow he found himself beginning to grin. The grin became a giggle, the giggle – a laugh and in a moment Denny – and his Dad were laughing uproariously; laughter full of irresponsibility, liveliness, sheer, ridiculous enjoyment.

Grace woke.

"'Ere, you alright?" she began, beginning to feel amused herself.

"I can't 'elp it!" he screamed helplessly and his intoxication reached out to Grace so that she too became overwhelmed. Their laughter echoed hysterically around the room deafening them to the sound of the street door opening; deafening then to the sound of a startled; "What the bloody 'ell!" from below. Deafening them to the sound of footsteps pounding up the stairs, three at a time, deafening them to the door handle turning, until the door itself burst open.

"My God, my bloody God!"

Denny turned, the laughter suddenly choking in his throat. Then he was harshly grabbed by Grace's father, hauled to his feet and felt the open hand of the ex-prizefighter explode against his face. The blow sent him sprawling painfully against the wall. George Manning looked at his daughter briefly:

"I'll deal with you later when I've finished murdering this bloody little sod."

This time he gave Denny a back-handed blow against his cheek, cutting Denny's face with his heavy gold signet ring. Denny forgot his nakedness, thought only of his pain, his life, this great ape suddenly spoiling his moment and as George's arm swung in the air to deliver another blow, he poised himself delicately, ducked the huge hand, and slammed his closed fist into the relaxing belly of his opponent. George bent double, with sudden astonishment on his face, and Denny seizing the advantage bunched his other fist and let rip against the big jaw. Incredibly the larger man was lifted off his feet, and he fell across the room hitting his head against the wardrobe. Grace leapt from the bed, her embarrassment forgotten.

"Oh my God, Denny," she screamed as she knelt by her father. "Denny, Denny, you've killed him, you've killed him!"

Denny gulped air and almost sobbing, ran alongside and stared down at the two figures. How glad Denny was to see the closed eyes slowly open.

"It's all right, love," said George, staring admiringly at his new discovery . . . "it's all right he only bloodywell knocked me for . . ."

* * * *

"SIX!"

Denny felt the aggression begin to flow through his body again; — you're young, you're strong – you can do it — he turned over onto his stomach and pushed himself up onto his knees. Instantly the throbbing in his ears became a deafening roar as the stadium erupted, exhorting Denny to "get up, get up, give us our money's worth —"

As Denny lifted his head he saw, with amazing clarity, Grace staring, her mouth wide open, tears streaming down her face, as though she were here with him . . .

* * * *

"SEVEN!"

". . . teen hours in labour. No wonder she was crying. He'd been sent out of the maternity room while the sister made yet another internal examination.

— Blimey what would George say if he knew I'd been up all night . . . he'd 'ave a fit . . . 'ruining your training schedule . . . six months of hard, solid workouts, free from that bloody sex-mad daughter of mine . . . and now you're jeopardising all that . . . think of that big little fight coming up. Think of the five years I've spent training you for this big moment. You'll be in the bigtime after this boy, no more money worries. You'll be able to see your mum all right – even find somewhere else for the old girl to live – somewhere posh . . ."

Denny chuckled to himself. As if she'd leave that little council flat after all this time. Suddenly he clutched his head . . .

— What am I doing laughing – Grace is in there going through bloody hell. I mustn't laugh I've got to think of her . . . give her some of my strength. Dear God, let her be all right, please let her be all right —

He thought of her tear-stained face lying on the pillow, her thick brown hair spread like blood, tangled, sweat-soaked. How different to the day he had married her. How long ago was it – four years, nine months, one week and two days . . . or was it three days now? She had looked fantastic that day, you'd hardly know she was three months pregnant. And George . . . what a turn-up. After he'd got over all his shocks, after he'd made sure that his jaw wasn't broken, he'd set about organising everything. The marriage, the wedding, the hospital, Denny's career prospects.

— "You've got everything going for you boy" he had said "you're young, not too young to get married so don't start having second thoughts, you've got a good physique, you're healthy, you've got a punch like a bloody mule kick, and if that weren't enough you've also got me to look after you and teach you everything I know."

And so it had been, with Denny's star rising fast and furiously leaving behind him a string of fallen comets terribly eclipsed by Denny's fast fists.

Yes, George had been wonderful. And how he idolised his grand-son Sammy, the product of Denny's first sexual experience. Abruptly Denny thought of his own father whom he'd last seen at the church on his wedding day. He'd been waiting anxiously for Grace to arrive, when a hand touched his shoulder. A cold shiver ran down his back as he'd turned . . . he hadn't recognised the shrunken, grey-haired figure at first. Then the man had smiled and the ageing was wiped out for a second.

"Hello, son."

"Dad?"

"Yes, it's me. Took you a while to recognise your old man didn't it? How are you son?"

Without waiting for a reply he continued.

"I saw your future-intended the other day."

"What . . . how?"

"I just called round to pay my respects like – see how you'd done. Don't worry, I didn't disgrace you or nothin'."

His father had grinned then, a boyish, lovable grin which had warmed Denny.

"I can see you've got your old man's taste. I'll just stay at the back of the church, see the ceremony. Won't embarrass you – and I'll just wish you luck now and God bless."

Then he had grasped Denny and hugged him.

"Don't tell your mum I was here – it might upset her. Good luck, boy."

Denny hadn't seen his father since then, but after each one of his fights he had received a telegram of congratulations and those Denny had kept and treasured.

The sister came through the gloomy swing doors, the face mask dangling below her chin like dead skin. Seeing the stricken look on Denny's face she smiled quickly.

"It'll soon be over, you can come in and give me a hand in a minute." She moved briskly into the office then and a moment later came out with an overall.

"Here, put this on, love . . ."

Denny hastily obeyed, feeling as though he were about to step out into space.

"Now the face mask . . . good lad . . . now then see that cylinder over there, be a dear and wheel it in for me – that wife of yours is using it up at a fair old rate."

Again Denny did as he was told. He entered the labour room, hardly daring to look at Grace. Then she moaned and he had to look. Her face was dead white and she looked completely sexless. Denny wheeled the cylinder to her side and fitted on the face mask as he had been shown.

"How are you feeling, love?"

Her eyes lifted weakly, then closed in a gesture which said everything.

The sister walked in, an assistant with her in attendance. They stood by the bed.

"Right, this is it now, Mrs Taylor. I want you to really push this time – I'm just going to give you a little injection down here which will ease the pain; and if we get into difficulties I'll give you a quick cut to make more room for the baby to come through – you won't feel a thing."

So the ordeal began again. Denny did his best to be a tower of strength but it was so different to that film he'd seen; and of course they hadn't let him see Sammy being born. All he could do now was grip Grace's hand, dab her soaking brow, and pass the face mask when necessary.

"Come on now, push dear, push . . ."

Grace, her back arched, her legs raised, pushed until the veins on her forehead were raised across her painfully wrinkled brow. Her teeth were set in a savage grimace and Denny trembled with a fear which he had never felt in the ring.

"We'll have to cut – get me the scissors nurse, quickly . . ."

Denny heard the snip-snip with horror, and Grace's screams pierced his brain . . .

"My Gawd, Denny, help me, help me . . .!"

* * * *

"EIGHT!"

* * * *

— pounds two ounces! "There, Mr Taylor, you've got a bonny baby girl . . . what you think of her?"

"She's beautiful," he said in a reverent whisper. Denny was still stunned by the last few moments. Almost immediately after the cut the baby had appeared; and Grace's pain and suffering were almost miraculously forgotten.

The baby was fantastic. He remembered that when he'd first seen Sammy, the boy had been wrinkled and brown like a pekinese almost and he had wondered if it was worth all the trouble. But thought his little creature's back was wrinkled her face and front were completely clear and she was wonderful to behold. Her head, unlike Sammy – who had been totally bald, was covered in a mass of dark, wet hair.

"Oh, Denny isn't she lovely?"

And seeing the wonderful smile on his wife's face caused him to . . . Jump to his feet on the count of . . .

* * * *

"NINE . . .!"

He could hear the crowd roaring encouragement as he steadied his trembling legs. The champion advanced, his relief suddenly diminished, knowing that he no longer had the strength to finish the kill.

Denny did enough to dodge the blows aimed at his head. Once the champion caught up with him, but Denny, remembering the tricks which George had taught him, embraced the champ, pinning his arms so that their punches were ineffectual; just for a second they were captured in that pose by the bright glare of a flash bulb – two lovers, sweat-soaked bodies entwined in a statuesque posture.

"Break!" and the moment was over, the seconds ticking away and the bell finally tolling for the champion but giving precious respite to the challenger. Denny walked to his corner. George was already there.

"Bloody 'ell, you left it late enough," was all he said, then he was brisk and business-like, attending to Denny's body.

"Last round coming up now boy, in spite of that last knockout, you great turd, you must be ahead on points – but go out there and get him if you can, otherwise it might be too close for comfort."

Denny didn't seem to hear. He turned to George:

"I love Grace."

"What the . . .?"

"I've never told her before . . ."

"Look, Denny don't worry about that now, tell her later, when you're the new champion."

Denny couldn't explain to George, but somehow he had had a vague sense of foreboding; it was this which had prompted him to blurt out; 'I love Grace . . .' as though he had to get the message across before it was too late.

"Seconds out"

George put a hand on Denny's shoulder.

"Good luck . . . son."

Their eyes met briefly and Denny saw the concern in George's face and felt sorry for him.

Then he was up on his feet advancing to the centre of the ring. Even as he advanced he knew that something was wrong; his eyes could not focus properly, there was an agonising pain at the base of his skull. The champion stretched out his gloved hands; Denny raised his and the two pairs of gloved hands touched. As they did so Denny's legs gave way and he saw a myriad of colours explode in front of his eyes; then he was down on the canvas with blood gushing from his ears, his nose and his mouth. There was the faintest hint of a smile on his face . . .

High Spirits

BY JANET MOODIE

Alice couldn't bear the damp, she pulled her cardigan tight around her for protection. Already she could feel her joints beginning to grind into a stiffening slowness, knuckles gnarled into a rigid curled grip. She looked at her hands, hands that had once be so dexterous and had obeyed her creative orders controlling the lightness of a sable brush, applying washes of delicate colour. She looked out at the fading landscape. Branches of the trees, now leafless, were shaggy with grey-green lichen that flourished in the hostile environment. She allowed herself some thought and wondered where hope had gone. She had come to the house full of hope and life, she thought she would have the time to spend on doing all those things she had dreamed of doing. Day by day her creativeness was etched away, her time was eaten by the gnawing demands of the house. She had hoped that now she had freed herself from domestic drudgery, she would be allowed to live the way she wanted to and not the way other people had dictated, but this was not so. Lackadaisical attitudes of un-professional botchers had worn away her dreams of getting things fixed. She was alone coping with leaking guttering, fused lights and leaning chimneys.

The incessant rain had been beating against the granite walls of the house all day. The house, remote and isolated, sat squarely in the earth. The defensive walls, now silvered with rain, held windows, squared in small panes of glass. Over the years, the house had been altered, yet its main part stood proud and solid, supporting its extensions and additions, suffering various occupiers and their ideas of enhancement. The land had been used originally for growing violets, but now the fields were neglected and returning to scrub land. Ivy and honeysuckle clung to the mortar of the remains of the walled garden, and on this wild November evening only the smell of smoke and sooty water lingered. Inside, strong beams supported its heavy cement-washed roof and the solid oak doors gàve an assuredness to the rooms. A cold basement housed a well so deep that a dropped pebble would resound into infinity. She stood for a while listening to the power of the storm. A miserable fire struggled in the sitting room grate, intermittently billowing out low hanging smoke that drifted into slow strands of soot which rested on freshly polished ledges.

Alice, nearly on the verge of tears, sighed with despair as she watched the rain accumulating into puddles on the floor of the granite fireplace. Kindling floated and paper sodden with sogginess, amassed in the wet black corners. She folded her arms, holding tight her secret emotions. Suppressing her fury and sadness zipped in with a tight downward mouth. Button bound she felt excluded from life in tortured isolation. The walls seemed her only protection yet she felt trapped by them unable to escape in case the house decided to crumble during her absence. The walls had become her jailer and she felt like a prisioner exiled, stranded, forgotten. Hermit like, she muttered to herself and answered the radio back, even arguing with it, putting it straight, putting it right.

A pan of soup chundered on the top of the Aga getting thicker as the afternoon light faded into darkness. She could hear buckets rattling around the yard as the wind tore at the outbuildings of the farm.

"They've stood up for three hundred years, I expect they'll still be there in the morning," she told the soup as she stirred.

Her mind dwelled on her situation. The place was too big for her to manage on her own, and there was no hope of any help. Her dreadful pride had manoeuvred her into this position, she had played the cards of life all wrong, been too much of a perfectionist, expecting everyone to do as she said, to be what she wanted them to be. But her pride had masked her weaknesses, covered over her vulnerability. In her desperation for love she had married a dreadful man, a domestic sadist and an infidel. Within that marriage she had nearly lost her identity, having to split herself into so many ways answering demands from children, husband, career. Always at someone's beck and call she lost her liberty and lived a life of unwarranted misery of duty and obligation. Until it came to her that she didn't have to live like that, she could do something about it. She didn't have to suffer the beatings and humiliation. It was then that the idea of Yew Berry pâté formed in her mind. Every time she suffered abuse at the hands of her husband the recipe formulated, and with the aid of the 'Robot Chef' and some lightly sautéd chicken livers enhanced with salt, butter and freshly ground pepper, she created the tempting deadly delicacy.

"The way to man's heart is through his stomach," Alice said chuckling at the memory. But where had it all led? At the time she had made a wonderful widow, lapping up the sympathy but now she was alone, isolated. Children all gone, youth, career, and hope all lost.

"It seems that I'm meant to be a domestic drudge. That must be my calling in life and it has taken me all this time for the realisation to dawn!" Alice muttered to herself as she knelt in the sooty wet hearth mopping up the rain water. Her hands were changing colour, grey was ingraining the cracks of the skin and camouflaging her red swollen knuckles.

"Where the devil did I get the idea that I was someone special? What makes me think that I've got any talent for anything. Everything is just a fantasy hope, and mine is no more." She wiped away some escaping hair from her face smearing it with sooty streaks then rested back onto her heels.

"I'm going to sell this place! Did you hear that you horrible house? I'm leaving you for someone else to worry about." Alice shouted the words so that every stone and beam heard it above the howling wind.

"Yes that is what I'll do! Sell it and get a few hens for company." She smiled to herself as the idea formulated in her mind. Feeling comforted by the soup she relaxed her set expression, she even un-buttoned her cardigan enjoying the comfort of self indulgence. Sitting in the smoke filled room she reflected on the day's events. None of her resolutions had been achieved. She had yet again been a slave to the house for the whole day, fixing one thing, cleaning another. No time for herself. No time for anything that she really wanted to do, like read a book or sketch the hills.

"This is no way to be going on." she said as she pulled the curtains on another day. "Tomorrow I'll get things sorted. Get things moving." The doors rattled as if they were trying to reply, attempting to argue, protesting. Momentary, in a chilled eerie silence, a strong smell of violets pervaded the smoke. Alice sniffed it, frowning with puzzlement, then she sniffed it again. Suddenly, there was an almighty crash! Alice stood rigid, fixed to the spot with only her eyes moving, darting from side to side in a silenced panic. Pale and dry mouthed, she slowly climbed the stairs. A cold breeze blew her wispy grey hair from its tight bound style and her heart pounded. With trepidation Alice entered the bedroom.

She stared with horror at the shattered glass that littered the floor and the pools of rainwater collecting on the deep recessed window ledge. Remnants of jagged glass remained in place surrounding a gaping night black hole through which the wind whistled.

A pain gripped Alice by the shoulders as the muscles at the back of her neck tightened. Her mouth set into its usual way as she took a deep breath and proceeded to carry out some kind of temporary repairs. Gathering her bedding into a bundle she wearily closed the door.

She entered an unused room which was filled with abandoned projects and things that were kept because they might be useful one day. Somewhere underneath the boxes of her children's outgrown toys, dusty Christmas decorations and broken chairs, she found her spare bed. She roughly spread out her bedding bundle and went down stairs.

"I've had enough for today, you can fall down for all I care," Alice screamed as her arthritic fingers gripped the tiny stopper of her hot water bottle. Slamming down the lid of the Aga, coal dust sparkled up with the sudden movement and the riddle iron crashed onto the slate hearth.

"Now look what you've made me do! Haven't you had enough of me today, what more do you want for God's sake, leave me alone."

The windows reverberated as if in answer and the walls seemed to shudder. Alice clutched her hot water bottle to her breast, folding her arms around its warmth and held up her head in defiance. A brightness came from the sitting room as the fire finally ignited into a rosy blaze dancing its shadows onto the walls and ceiling. Alice laughed aloud.

"Success at last. You needn't think you're getting the better of me. She tossed a defiant head as she went to the cellar for some logs. Then a creak, then a slam, as the sound of the closing door echoed around the blackness.

"No!" Alice screamed. But nobody heard.

A Man of Few Words

BY JOHN T. WILSON

It was cold that winter before the war and the sudden squalls of January brought hail scudding in over the Atlantic breakers as often as they brought rain.

She liked it then, snuggled under the eiderdown in the cottage bedroom, her lover by her side. Her husband, surly and uncouth, would be sheltering in some pigs' craw on the croft where he belonged. He kept to a strict routine, unmoved by hail, rain or the rare snowfalls which turned the black carns she hated into something almost beautiful.

It was with a sense of outrage, then, half-dressed in the kitchen, that she faced him when he returned unexpectedly while her lover, the landlord of the village pub, lay scared, upstairs in her bed. She felt that her husband had no right to be home halfway through the morning and her sin paled into insignificance before his violation of the fixed routine of their days.

"What do you want?" she had demanded aggressively.

Her husband was a man of few words.

"He be upstairs, then?" he stated, more than asked.

"And what if he is?" she retorted, anger her best defence, jeering, "You've not been interested in me for a long time!"

"So it's true" said the farmer heavily. "You'll stop seeing him. Get him out of here before I take my shotgun to the pair of you!"

Her refusal surprised even her and his response, final and abrupt, gave her a tingling sense of anticipated freedom.

"All right," he had said, "if you're set on shaming us in the eyes of the whole parish with your fancyman from the pub I'll not stop you. I'm going. I ask only this, that in a year's time you'll ring this number. Promise me that."

She promised and he went from the kitchen and was never seen in the parish again. The landlord of the village pub, her lover, moved in and the scandal slowly settled, though was never forgotten, as it could not be in the tiny parish where generations of dark Cornish farmers had wrested a living from the granite rocks under the bleak hills.

The year passed and the lovers' passions cooled, speeded by the bouts of unexplained illness that dogged them in that cottage where illicit love had burned its bright and splendid sun. By the end of the year, the publican lover in hospital with gastro-enteritis, she herself, racked by pains, drawn and ill, remembered her promise.

She rang the number her husband had given her and found it to be a firm of local soliciters.

"Yes" said the senior partner, "I have a letter for you, to be handed over next Friday." It was a year to the day her husband had left.

She sat wide-eyed at the scrubbed kitchen table as the thin winter sun illuminated the sheet of paper he had left her.

"I will never leave you" he had written, "You will find me in the water tank."

Occam's Razor

BY BETTY BEYER

The eighth day. Monday, 8th July. Eight days since Sonia went missing. I count carefully, double-checking for error. Any slip could put Frank into further danger. I watch every statement I make. As they watch – the police. They are out there now.

It is late, but the long summer nights are warm. The tourists linger on the beaches. Here in the centre of town the pubs in Market Square are full, and the tables and chairs outside crowded. It will soon be closing time and quieter. I sit in my room and wait.

The blue car, Inspector Lake's car is parked in Quarry Road, a bit away from the corner, but I can see it from my bedroom window. They don't watch all night, do they? I go over it again and again in my mind.

Day 1 July 1st.

It was a Monday. Weekends were always the worst for Frank; the constant rows, the recriminations. Sometimes she was hysterical and talked about me as 'that witch, that scheming deceitful bitch.' But she couldn't prove anything. We were very discreet.

I was sitting at my desk with a pile of recent additions to catalogue. I like my work. The public sees librarians as poetic and literary. But cataloguing is a logical skill, as precise as mathematics. I do not like to be interrupted.

He tapped on my door respectfully, and came in, closing it behind him.

"What's wrong, love?" I asked at once. He looked as if he had not slept.

"It's Sonia. She's gone" he said. "We had the most terrible row. She knows, she knows about us." His voice was rising in panic.

"Take it easy," I said, "and keep your voice down. Sit there for a minute. What do you mean gone? Gone where?"

"She stormed out. She took her coat and handbag, and . . ." he hesitated "her pills, her sleeping pills."

"She'll be back" I said. "You know what she's like. She's probably gone to her parents." I thought of the big house, Penlea, on the wide reaches of the Helford river, with its own shingle beach and the stone boathouse. No wonder Sonia was discontented in their grubby flat, with nothing to do but nurse her neuroses; discontented in spite of the gifts of sports car and flash clothes from her doting father.

"No, she's not there. Anyway her parents are away; in Greece, I think. I phoned, there was no reply."

"She could be in the house and not answering." I said. "That would be just like her. Look," I leaned over and touched his hand. "We can't talk here. Let's have lunch together, just for once." He fiddled with the edge of the desk.

"I've got to take the van to Helford today. I'll be out till four. Come to my place tonight. Come to the flat. Please come," he begged. He was eager, excited.

"I can't come there," I said. "She might turn up at any moment. Anyway I don't like it, not in her space." I had been there once, when Sonia was abroad, but had always regretted it. But my flat was out of the question; not in this small town, and with my job.

"No she won't," he said with extraordinary conviction. "Phone first if you like, but she won't come."

I went, against my better judgement. It was a weird evening. Frank was slightly drunk when I got there, unusual for him so early in the evening. It was like a celebration. He had made a meal, a good one too, with all the trimmings, candles and a cheap bubbly wine. I couldn't believe it.

He kissed me rapturously and plied me with drink. Soon we were reaching for each other, the meal half-eaten. We fell into bed. At first I jumped at every sound.

"She won't come," he kept saying, "and if she does I don't care." Afterwards we dozed a little.

When we woke later, his mood had evaporated, and mine with it.

"Three years," he wailed, "three years with a maniac. She tried to kill me, you know, with the butcher's knife. You don't believe me, do you? Well, she did?"

We made love again, desperately. I held his soft curls against my breast and wished I could comfort him. Yet I knew him too well to imagine he would make the break. Sonia's money, her parents' money erased his fears, his deep sense of insecurity. Oh yes, he loved me, but he feared poverty more.

He climaxed again, and then turned away, relaxing into sleep. How could he? My ears were stretched for the slightest sound.

"What if she comes back?" I asked.

"She'll kill us, I expect," he said, half-laughing. "The knife is still on the coffee table. Don't touch it will you?"

"Why ever not, for God's sake," I asked crossly.

"Evidence," he mumbled sleepily. Coyly he elaborated. "Her fingerprints. They'll be on the handle." I dismissed this as drunken nonsense.

"Come on," I said. "Sober up and do something or I'm going."

"No, don't do that," he said in alarm. "Don't leave me alone here." He got out of bed and pushed a chair under the door handle.

"There," he gestured dramatically. "That should hold her. She won't manage to stab us in our sleep."

"Don't talk such rubbish," I said. "She'll be back in the morning; she's probably crying her eyes out at Mary's." I left at four, restless and hung over. Frank woke as I got out of bed. I listened but he didn't replace the chair after I had closed the door.

Day 2 Tuesday

He appeared late at work, looking green and tense. Fortunately the mobile van was in for stocktaking. I avoided his eyes as he apologised to Mason. A little flutter went round the stock room. I overheard odd words as I inspected the laminating on the latest batch of paper-backs. 'The police' and 'missing', 'worried about her state of mind.' There were a few giggles and sly looks; Sonia had had more than one jealous tantrum on that very spot. Frank had always had an eye for a pretty face. That's putting it politely – 'a nice ass' was his expression. But I doubt if anyone could have guessed what erotic thrills the staid Miss Maurice had given to little boy Frank!

We were scrupulous all day. My phone rang just as I got home. "Come and see me," he pleaded. But I said no. It was alka-seltzers, bath and bed for me, although I didn't tell him so. The young seem to be immune to fatigue.

"She'll be home before the police find her," I comforted him. "Did you tell them that you'd had a row? Domestic, they'll call it, and just make soothing noises."

"I said we'd had a little tiff." he said in an odd cold voice.

Wednesday evening, 3rd July

We met at his place, cold-eyed and sober this time. He looked ghastly. No news. Nothing from the police. He drank too much but I did not join him. He seemed pre-occupied and I felt piqued. After all on the phone he had begged me to come. At one point he said "Perhaps you shouldn't be here; but I don't suppose they'd come in the evening, would they?"

"Who might come? Her parents are in Greece, aren't they? Anyway on Monday you said you didn't care. At least we're fully clothed and respectable tonight." He looked surprised.

"Not them; the police, I mean. They wouldn't come in the evening on routine matters, would they to search the flat?" He had moved the butcher's knife, I noticed; replaced it in the slot in the rack on the kitchen wall.

"Look," I said, "you're not making any sense. You'll have to sort it out. You can't expect the police to do everything. Why don't you take the day off tomorrow. I can square it for you. I'll say you phoned me. Go up to Penlea and see if she's there. Have you phoned Mary? or George Hanna, or her old flat-mate in Chelsea?" He looked hard at me.

"I don't want to find her," he said. My heart ached for his little-boy helplessness.

"Oh, my dear, I know you don't but we can't leave it like this, can we? Find her and break with her properly. Then we can be together."

"Where would I live?" he accused. "You know the flat is hers. You won't have me at your place." He turned aside, muttering, "too soon, I don't want to find her too soon." Did he say 'soon,' or 'not too soon'? "The police will find her." he went on.

"What did you say?" I asked

"Nothing, nothing, what do you care?" he whimpered drunkenly.

It was too much after all I'd risked. It was useless with him maudlin. I rounded on him, and told him in no uncertain terms what I thought of his spinelessness. Then I stormed out. Only as I sat in my Mini, tremblingly fitting the key in the ignition did I contemplate that I might have lost him.

Thursday

He rang me distractedly at 8.00 a.m. as I sat toying with my breakfast. My spirits soared at his voice.

"Please, please help me," he begged. "The police are coming to the flat at two this afternoon. I must clean up. I must. There's something I've got to tell you. You've got to help me."

I went cold. The pieces fell into place. Unthinkable; it only happened in books. But it *had* happened, to someone I knew, to Frank. He had killed her. That's why he was so sure she wouldn't come back. He poured his love into my ear.

"You're strong, Miss Mouse, you're the only one who can help me, the only one who cares."

I telephoned the library to say I had a migraine; a rare event, Miss Maurice off sick. I said Frank had phoned to say the police needed him for their enquiries. I only hoped no-one would connect the two happenings.

When I got to the flat he was distraught.

"I thought they'd find her first and not need to look here." He was mopping the kitchen floor with over-soapy water, suds everywhere. On the draining board was a white towel, dust-soiled as if dragged on the floor. I lifted it by one corner. The centre was stained with blood, darkened and stiffening now. A lot of blood.

I took the mop from his hand, found the bottle on the sideboard and poured us both a whiskey. I needed one as much as he did.

"Tell me what happened. Tell me where she is . . ." I shuddered "where the body is." He lifted his head in surprise.

"I didn't kill her," he said indignantly. "I *didn't* kill her. I told you. She came at me with the knife." He was breathing hard. "I held her wrists. She kicked my shins. They're black with bruises. When she saw she couldn't get at me she went quiet. She had the knife in her hand." He winced at the memory. "Then she drew it across her arm."

I refilled his glass. He was trembling. He went on.

"There was a lot of blood. She must have fainted; she fell on the floor. I wrapped the towel round it, and then got some plaster strips to put on it. She moaned and groaned a bit but she didn't stop me. Then I carried her in here and put her in that chair; where you're sitting," he added morosely. He looked at me.

"Do you believe me now?" he asked. I avoided the question.

"What happened then?" I said.

"It looked as if it needed some stitches, so I went into the hall to phone Dr. Alexander. He knows her; wouldn't make too much fuss."

"Did you speak to him?" I asked eagerly.

"No, the line was engaged." He was still looking at me questioningly. "As I got back she was picking up her coat and handbag. 'I'll get you' she said 'I'll *get* you! Then she walked out of the door." He drank the rest of his whiskey and held out his glass for more. "She took her sleeping pills, but not her lithium tablets. She'll be spaced out by now. She took her car; you know how she drives, Lynne. God knows what she's done by now." I stared at him, unbelieving.

"You didn't go after her?" I asked.

"No," he said evenly, "no, I didn't follow her."

It was the same thing, I reflected, the same thing as murdering her. I knew then that he was capable of cruelty.

"The cut?" I asked, turning my bare forearm to him. "Was it like this?" I placed two fingers across the blue veins at my wrist.

"No," he said softly. "I pulled the knife away. More like this." He drew a line with his index finger, diagonally across to his inner elbow.

"Why didn't you tell the police all this?"

"How could I?" he replied crossly. "You don't believe me. Do you imagine they would?"

I left the flat well before lunch, carrying the towel in a plastic bag. It's in my airing cupboard now, bleached and boiled but with still a faint brown stain in the centre. 'Occam's Razor' I ruminated in my own bed that night. I had just come across the phrase in a reference volume on philosophy. 'Occam's Razor: Given a set of facts, the connection between them is likely to be the most obvious one. If I walk under an apple tree and an apple falls on my head, then first I deduce that it has fallen off the tree. Of course it may have been thrown from a nearby window. In any murder case the most likely suspect is always the spouse.

When they found her body; if they found her body? Well anyone can move a body, fake a suicide. But what if he was telling me the truth? Then she would turn up some time, and the less he said now the better. I might question his ethics but I could not fault his logic. And now, with the police involved I dare not contact him again.

FRIDAY, Day 5

Back to work for both of us, but I did not see him; only a glimpse as he loaded the mobile for the long run to the villages of West Penrith. By 9.30 the big white vehicle with its bold lettering had pulled out of the yard. A long quiet day.

By six in the evening I sat at home, desperate for a phone call. I regretted my coldness, was full of plans. All I wanted was to see him again. I would take a bottle of brandy. We would lie together in the shadowy bedroom, lie in each other's arms and comfort one another. Of course he hadn't done it.

Four days now. Either . . . or something must have happened. Something awful, or something more mundane. Maybe she'd flown to Greece. Maybe she'd left him for good and was fixing up a flat in London with Daddy's money.

He was in a callbox on the Helston road; had a flat on the return run and had to call the garage out. He sounded tired and offhand.

"I'm coming over to your place; I'll make a meal for us." I coaxed.

"You'd better not. Don't go there." he commanded. He sounded alarmed. "She might come back while you are there. She'll be furious." he went on. I could tell he was lying. He often did; he had a special voice for it. My anger boiled over.

"Come back? you know she won't come back." I shouted. There was a long pause.

"Look here . . ." he began.

"I am looking, I am looking." I raged. "You know she won't come back. You killed her. You murdered her." Did I believe it or did I just say it? He sounded shocked, injured.

"You're talking rubbish. Get a hold of yourself," he said. His voice was very cold. I was indignant. Me get a hold of myself? After his moans and tears? I slammed down the receiver.

I sat and let the tears flow. It was as if I was paralysed; I could not move my body from that place. My mind swung pendulum-like between belief in his story, his feeling for me, to the blackest rage and fear.

An hour passed. I heard the church clock strike seven. When it did ring again the phone bell startled me. I grasped it eagerly, all my love overflowing. He spoke my name.

"I'm sorry, my dearest; it was a hideous thing to say, to think . . ." He did not wait for me to finish.

"She's been back," he said breathlessly. She's been to the flat. She's taken some slacks and her thick shoes" he groaned, "and the butcher's knife. It's gone." In spite of myself relief flooded over me. The heady drama of the last few days was over. She was alive.

"Look, love," I said. "This time you must find her. Try Penlea first; and tell the police – about the knife, I mean. She's only taken it to frighten you. Do it now. And ring me absolutely as soon as you can, won't you? Promise, promise." I insisted. His voice came back short and odd.

"You believe me now, then?" Afterwards it was that, that last remark that made me doubt him.

The evening was endless, but I felt better. I pottered, feeding myself, doing odd jobs. By eleven I sat by the phone with a drink. I waited for news. He'd find her and bring her home. He'd put her to bed with pills and then he'd phone me. Or he would not find her. He would not go on looking all night.

I waited till midnight. No call. I waited till one. Then I rang him. No reply. The phone rang and rang in an empty room. I rang again and again, every ten minutes till two in the morning. Then I could stand it no more. I had the key, from three nights ago.

There were no lights in the window as I drove up. Opening the front door made my flesh creep. Silence. The kitchen door was ajar; the sitting room deserted. A newspaper lay in my path on the floor. I picked it up and threw it on to the settee. At the bedroom door, absurdly, I knocked. No sound. The room was empty; perfume, expensive perfume strong on the air. It had not been there on that wild and drunken night. I crossed to the dressing table and picked up the small spray bottle. Gingerly, turning the nozzle away I pressed. It was her perfume, but too much. Novelettish. Anyone could spray perfume in a room; anyone could take away slacks and shoes. And the butcher's knife?

I shuddered. What if she were not dead yet? Was it some sort of plot, an alibi, a way of confusing the time of death? I drove away aimlessly through the empty streets. I must know, one way or the other. From habit I found myself outside the library, our only other place of contact. We both had keys to the side door, to the stock-room. We had met there sometimes. I found myself blushing at memories of uncomfortable love-making on the hard floor.

I was right. On my desk a propped envelope with his handwriting, sealed and marked in bold letters 'Personal.' Inside a leaf pulled from my scrap pad, a cryptic note. It read: 'Meet me at the boathouse, Monday night, late. Not before Monday.' 'Late' was underlined. 'Not before Monday' was underlined twice.

It was something. Not before Monday? But of course he did not know that I would read it before Monday. I did not work on Saturdays. The boathouse was one of our trysting places, a place where we had often met. There was even a bed there, a narrow canvas bed. We had looked up sometimes to the lights of Penlea, excited by our daring. Oddly comforted, I drove home.

On Saturday, day six, I did not go out. At three in the afternoon my doorbell rang. I ran down the stairs, not caring who saw us. Through the inner door two figures were outlined. I could have cried with disappointment. Two men in dark suits stood outside.

"Miss Maurice are you Miss Lynne Maurice?" the taller man asked.

"Yes, I am," I replied abruptly.

"Inspector Lake." He took out a plastic-covered identity card and waved it under my nose. "And this is Sergeant Williams. Could we come in for a few minutes? It's about a colleague of yours, Mr. Frank Hastings. He reported his wife missing on Tuesday." Quickly turning my head away I moved towards the stairs.

"Of course," I answered. "but I don't know him very well – just through work." The sergeant closed the front door carefully and they followed my. "My flat is upstairs. Do come up." I said as calmly as I could. Once inside I sat them in chairs, offered them coffee which they refused, and tried to collect my wits.

The Inspector began smoothly.

"You don't know where he is, do you? His plans for the weekend?" I looked surprised.

"No," I replied. "I know he's worried about his wife, that's all. She's ill, you know."

"You know his wife, then?"

"Well, yes, by sight, and I have spoken to her. She picks him up at work sometimes." I was careful with the tense.

"But she's not a friend of yours by any chance?" I frowned.

"No, not at all." I answered coldly.

"You've never been to their flat, then?" He made the statement, and moved swiftly on. "You see, Mr. Hastings said he'd meet us at his flat this morning. We wanted to make a further search. Just routine, you know. Sometimes something in the home: a letter, a diary entry and an expert can judge the state of mind, can see it more clearly than someone close."

Alarm bells rang in my head – 'search – fingerprints.' I broke in quickly.

"Wait a minute. I've just remembered. I did call there once. To give him a changed work schedule. He drives the mobile library, you know, and for the long runs he leaves early, before the library opens."

"How long ago might that have been?" he asked quietly. I stammered.

"I don't know – a week or two maybe." He looked me full in the eye.

"This week?"

"Oh, no," I said, shocked. "No".

"Was she there with him when you called?" I could see Sergeant Williams writing swiftly in his notebook as I answered.

"Oh, yes, they were both there."

"Then you won't mind coming down for fingerprinting." He paused, watching me tremble. He said, kindly. "There'll be lots of friends' prints in the flat. We'll be looking for strange ones." He turned to the sergeant with a nod. The notebook was closed.

"Is there anything else you'd like to tell us?" he asked gently. "And if you do think of anything you'll let us know, of course." I remembered the whiskey bottle and the coffee cups.

"I think they gave me a drink." I said. I wanted them to write that down but they didn't.

I saw then out politely. I was shaking. The summer heat was intense; I could hardly walk up the stairs. Dosed with aspirin and with a cold pack to my head I lay down in my darkened room and dozed and dozed through the rest of the day. I could only wait. I must go to work on Monday as if nothing had happened. Till Monday night, Monday night, late. He needed me at the boathouse. Sonia's parents had a boat, and the big outboard motor was in the double garage at the house. The key was on Sonia's key-ring.

We could go up or down the coast, and out from another port. I saw myself as Ethel le Neve to his Crippen, only I'd make a better boy. Was that too fanciful? Had I read too many thrillers?

All through the bitter long weekend, all that day and Sunday too I moved in a daze of speculation, a creature turning and turning on a wheel in a cage.

Till now, Monday night, late.

I waited a long time, sitting unmoving in my chair. I drank a brandy, poured another. The radio played on quietly. Then the blue car was gone from the corner.

I was ready. Slacks, stout shoes. No luggage, only a bulging handbag, with money and my passport. Soon I was on the road to Tregenna Head. I parked far off the highway, well down the bumpy track. I scrambled quickly down the familiar path. The cove was beautiful in the warm darkness. Faint light shone on the still water; the far bank was veiled in mist and darkness as it widened to the sea. My eyes became accustomed to the light. As I approached I knew with a sudden excitement that my surmises were right. My footsteps must have been audible, my shoes clattering gently, moving the flat pebbles and sea-washed shingle. The faintest smell of salt and seaweed mingled with the fragrance of warm grass. The door of the boathouse was ajar and moving slowly. In spite of it all, the horror, the doubts, love and yearning rose in me and I ran to him, aching to be held in his arms.

The door opened wider. I stopped dead with a sickening lurch, struggling to keep my balance on the piled stones. I fought with a giddiness that threatened to overwhelm me. Ghosts? Apparitions? But no, my senses did not fail me. She was thinner, with a wildness of eye, her hoarse voice pouring out incoherence, foul-mouthed with obscenity. There was a raw puckered scar across her fore-arm. It was Sonia.

I pushed past her, shining my torch around the boathouse, sweeping the floor and walls to the corner and the little bed. A strong stench hit me, of overheated kitchens, of stale food, meat and blood, bone-tainted. One glance and I knew he was dead. Huddled face to the wall I saw the lines of the brown linen jacket that I loved him to wear. His knees were drawn up to his chest like a crouching child; he hugged to himself the handle of the missing butcher's knife. Bright blue patterned socks, old scuffed sandals. No flesh was visible, only the back of his head, the curly brown hair I loved to fondle. No flesh except for one hand. His arm was flung backwards, turned outward from the elbow, resting lightly on the canvas-covered strut of the camp bed. Not his warm, familiar caressing hand; this hand was leaden, fingers curled like stiff petals, cupping the pool of dried blood in the upturned palm.

They had not been far behind me: Inspector Lake, the sergeant, men in plain clothes, some in uniform. Dr. Alexander held Sonia as she shrieked and shrieked with animal intensity.

I could not have done it, of course, could not have turned that loved body towards me, touched those soft curls, cradled his face one last time between my palms. But what is left for me, as memory, as reproach for the bitter thoughts of the last week? Only a nightmare glimpse of a dark corner in a stone-built boathouse, the beam of a torch, a silent figure, face turned to the wall on a rough camp bed.

But that was not the worst of it. Then I did not know one half of the horrors that lay in store for me.

Sonia was the undoubted star of her own trial. Dressed always in black, with sometimes a touch of white for purity at her throat, she held the gaze of the predominantly male jury of Cornishmen: staunch pillars of the chapel, lusty male voice singers, fishermen in cold waters. They stared mesmerised at her cloud of dark hair, the lift of her pale face, strained to hear her painful whispered replies. Delicate, a wronged wife, deceived and cheated by a philanderer, they adored her.

The experts in psychiatry glossed over her snivelling adolescent history, talked of strain beyond endurance for a passionate and tender soul. She's cosily tucked up now in a soft prison, waiting for a favourable psychological re-assessment, and no doubt parole in a few years.

And me? They crucified me at the trial. The prosecution pulled my statement apart. Only an acquaintance? Just called at the flat? And why, then, were there fingerprints on the perfume bottle, the switch of the bedside lamp? Why was the Mini parked outside till four in the morning?

And what happened on Saturday, day six, that endless relentless day? They think he died in the early hours of that morning. They cannot tell me if he was struck while resting on that final bed, or crawled in agony to huddle there for his last hours.

And why the note, why 'Monday late, not before Monday.'?

It seems that sweet Carol Stebbing, she of the dark eyes and schoolgirl blushes, she of the afore-mentioned 'nice ass' was at the 'George' in nearby Porthleven, with a cosy double bedroom booked in the name of Carter. Like me on that Friday night, she waited and waited for Frank, spending the evening in the lounge bar, looking up every time the door opened. Eventually she slept tearfully alone in the double bed, leaving after breakfast. Her father later had to cover the cheque she wrote to pay the bill.

After that I ceased to care. No use now to feel defiant, no use to think, if only, if only! No, there is nothing. Not even one last look; only a nightmare glimpse of a huddled figure, clutching a knife to his breast, his face turned towards the wall.

Shadow Play

BY DILYS GATOR

Sitting in the deep bay window that juts out over where the steps go down to the sea. High tide, it seems to lap at the very foundations of the house, each ebb and flow wearing away the solid rock so that I can see, almost in an eye-blink, that eternal patience crumbling the last fragment, the house collapsing, being swallowed up. Or only the echo of the house. It won't be there then.

Now, though, it is present, it is real. Window-seat with padded chintz cushions supports me; glass is cold against my nose; velvet hangings are soft to my touch. I look at my hand, lifted to stroke the claret-coloured draperies. My hand. This strange, bony appendage with blue veins and gawky knuckles. It doesn't look like my hand, but it is. I exist. I live. This is my hand, I tell myself.

I stare at it for a few moments, wondering, then let it drop, pick up the pen and notebook beside me and turn from the grey day outside, the fog heavy with fine droplets of water that cling to the window panes, the presence of the sea muted, invisible. Here there is warmth, the reassurance of thick red carpets, the spaciousness of the high ceiling, the cream walls with mirrors catching the light in prisms and throwing it back and forth, from side to side.

TODAY, THE FUTURE STARTS.

I pause, consider the words I have written. It depends whether you have a positive or a negative attitude. Today is the watershed, the line between what has gone and what will come. Today the future starts, but today, equally certainly, the past ends. Unborn tomorrow, said Omar, and dead yesterday. And in between, the shifting seconds of now.

I rise, go across to one of the mirrors, stare at myself with impersonal curiosity. How boring to see the same face every time I look in a mirror. I twist my head to try and catch an angle of myself that I have never seen before, some small glimpse to relieve the dullness bred by familiarity. It doesn't work. It never works. Always the same me that looks back.

How old is my face? Time means nothing to the soul. Age is just a word. Every year of my life I have looked different, but to myself I am always the same. Trapped in the now of the present. Maybe even memory is an illusion. I think about Time. The ticking of my watch, the beat of my heart. On and on, for ever and ever. Yet each tick, each beat, is the only one that exists. The last has slipped into the past; the next may never happen. How slender is the thread. We live always in the moment of awareness. What is real may change by the time we draw another breath. Where was I, a heart-beat ago? Now I am here, but where was I then? I cling to the reality of my own pulse, afraid in sudden panic that it may stop. I feel the blood pounding in my head so that I can see nothing. Feel the dimensions sliding from my grasp. Run from the room in smothering terror, calling:

"Edwin. Edwin?"

Where the hell is he? Anger stabs through me. He should be here when I need him. He's here often enough when I don't, when I want to be left alone. Hovering, protecting, caring, until I could scream.

His voice floats up from the depths of the hall below the wide, shallow stair-case.

"Is that you, pigeon?"

Emerging from the study doorway, bald head shining, shirt-sleeves neatly confined by old-fashioned gold cuff-links, brown spaniel's eyes watching me anxiously as I go down the stairs.

"Is something the matter?"

The reality of smooth wood under my hands has brought me back. The terror is gone, and the anger is taking on form. It's settled on Edwin's baldness, his stockiness, and specially the concern in his eyes. I feel such revulsion that I know I have to get away.

"I thought I'd go for a walk," I say, through stiff lips.

"In this fog?" he says doubtfully, just as I knew he would. Irritation sharpens my voice. This is a familiar ritual.

"Why shouldn't I go for a walk?"

He sighs.

"I'm busy as the moment, but I'll come for a walk with you later."

Is it worth the effort of arguing, asserting myself? This morning, I haven't got the strength. I say nothing.

"Why don't you go and do some writing?" he suggests, and mutely, heavy-limbed, I turn and begin the climb to the top floor and the cliche Edwin's faithfully observed – the attic converted into a "work-room" where I have spread out my papers and books, typewriter and pen. Stiff with resentment, I shut the door behind me, reject Edwin, reject the world. I don't want to write. I feel tired, exhausted. I sit on the big patchwork cushion on the floor, lean against the wall, curl myself up small, think about living and dying.

* * * *

Man, said Rousseau, is born free, but is everywhere in chains. Huddled on the cushion, I wonder about freedom, about chains. Was I born free? A free spirit with free will? Or was it all predestined, my path laid out for me? Were the chains already waiting even as I was laid in Maeve's arms for the first time? Could I have broken away, smashed the bonds that linked me in my small dependency to the two creatures who had fashioned my earthly body from their own?

Could I have piped infant defiance into Maeve's face or denied those other hands, that, in their male strength, protected his child from scavengers? Should I have somehow realised the enormity of his crime, recognised the dark wings beating round my head when, a scavenger himself, he swooped from the clouds to violate, even as the tears streamed down his face, the flesh of his own living lamb?

The weakness was in him, not in me, yet it was round the mind of his child that the chains grew tighter, the trap closed. Should I have, with atavistic wisdom beyond my years, passed judgement on him, pronounced sentence, cut through my chains with an epigram and left him kneeling, shamed yet still assured of his soul's salvation if he confessed in humility the frailties of his flesh?

"Mea culpa," he weeps, through his fingers, his gaze turned inward to the dark, secret, ecstatic sin. And Maeve beside him, her hair a cloud, the nails of a martyr's cross bleeding from her unseeing eyes where they have pierced the soul and life is dripping away.

"Mea culpa." Meave forms the words with her lips.

For them the richness of the ruby lamp, gold stars, penitence thick as incense on the air, abasement, chastisement, absolution. But the unspoken reality grows in the womb of their child like a monstrous cancer, until the time comes when it breaks forth into hideous form, splitting the shell that has carried the burden for so long.

Red slashes across my wrists released that devouring spectre of guilt into my own image, my shadow, my shape, my doppelganger. It was a confrontation sealed with blood. "I am you and you are me. You can never escape me. I will never leave you." I can see her clearly, myself, my other self, her white skin charred, festering. She is laughing across from the mirror, even as I hide my eyes. I can hear her laughter beating from the four walls, beating me down, battering me to the floor.

"Let me die. Oh, God, let me die."

But instead I feel those familiar hands that fathered both her and me, a travesty of tenderness. I hear Maeve's scream splintering the air into a million shattered pieces. God is Love. Love is his hands, his lips, his voice, and Maeve's prostrate body weeping tears that will never end for my soul. Love is the stain of my guilt, the image in the mirror that haunts me as I run from room to room, the sin that laughs down the corridors of memory like a scratched old record on the turntable of Time, playing itself in my head until I beat myself again and again at the floor so that my pain may silence it.

God is Love. God is Infinite. God is everywhere. There is no escape. But later comes the cleansing, the purging of my spirit. The realisation that I can leap the bounds of reality, forsake the substance for the shadow. I can see through the mirror. I see Lucifer strong and magnificent, the throne of God beneath him shrivelling. I see that black is white, that dark is light, that day is night. I am Judas, giving the kiss of love to my betrayer. I know myself, I am the image behind the glass, I am the alter ego cast by the sun, that runs on the ground and crawls with the worms. Nothing can confine me. I have found my freedom.

* * * *

Chained then, but I am free as air. I am travelling from nowhere into nothing. I have no roots to pull me down. I never speak of the house in London, I do not want to remember it. And I have denied Maeve's memories of Ireland, wiped out the sound of her voice as, a third in our dark trinity, she mourned that I had tempted him, that I made him fall. I have rejected the prayers that insinuated themselves into my dreams, the earnest pleading for my salvation.

Maeve blamed herself because that was in her nature, and she blamed me because I was the reincarnation of that self, but not wispy and insubstantial, something formed from the mists and glimmers on lake water, dimmed through hours on her knees, weeping. I was the Maeve she might have been once, hair softly curling round white shoulders, eyes with their sooty lashes so deeply blue that they smote your heart. Not a wraith, but a vivid and vital being of fire, an enchantress. She never blamed him. It was her fault, and it was mine, because I was her daughter and in spite of my unawareness, my innocence, the pattern played itself through a second time, and once again he was too weak to resist.

So I have no country. I am a wanderer. I can go where I please and do what I will. There is no Time for me. I regulate it myself, create my own days and nights.

Here, though, in this house, Edwin's reality rules me, as it did in the house in Hampstead where he and Mrs Edwards and the ghost of his mother had established their rituals long before he married me. Edwin and Mrs Edwards and the ghost of his mother cling manically to the chains of their lives. Familiar. Comfortable. A place for everything, and everything in its place. An evening for cleaning the silver, which must never vary. After I broke a cup from the Doulton tea-service, I was not allowed to wash up again.

"You don't need to, pigeon. Mrs Edwards would rather do it, as she has always done. You don't need to do anything."

"But Edwin, I'd like to think I was being useful."

His smile, indulging a child.

"You're a writer, you don't have to be useful. And after all, you're not strong yet, you've got to get well. I'll see to everything. Just don't you worry your head about anything except your poems."

Smothering, feeling the weight of yet another love grinding me down, stifling me, I accepted the burden and nodded. How hard is resignation when one's protest is not against evil but good; not against injustice but benevolence; not against starvation but a surfeit of sweetness.

In spite of his love for me, his devotion, even my physical presence is an intrusion. His mother's ghost still presides over the household. The mahogany-and-stuffed-velvet chairs that stand round the table in the dining-room looking out over the sea, stood just so in the Hampstead house. The mirrors on the walls are filled with her image, her secretive smile. Mrs Edwards unfailingly washes, cleans, tidies as though a phantom finger will be run across surfaces looking for dust, a phantom frown pucker that imperious brow if there is a single deviation from the ritual established in the hollow, claret-draped rooms of the Hampstead house when, a red-cheeked wench from the country, Clara Dew as she was then, she tearfully attempted to accept her new life "in service".

After a while, her longing for green fields and apple blossom quivering in the spring sunlight, laughter in crystal droplets like spilled water from the pump, faded. Maybe there was a renewal of life when she managed to become Clara Edwards; maybe she hoped the colours would come back into her world of coal-scuttles and blacking and morning teas served behind heavy drawn curtains, the egg boiled for exactly two-and-a-half minutes, or else the spoon would be laid down without comment, but there would be no escaping the accusation in those eyes.

Maybe, but the face that smiles from the frame in her room, cap tilted jauntily as though to defy Air Force Regulations, was blown to pieces over the Channel. Sometimes Mrs Edwards plays Vera Lynn singing 'We'll Meet Again' and 'The White Cliffs of Dover' on her old cabinet gramophone, and enjoys an evening of tearful nostalgia. But using the right serving spoons with the vegetable dishes brings more balm to Mrs Edward's soul than anticipating reunion with the laughing-eyed and shattered face within the frame.

A sea-gull has alighted noisily outside the little gable window, on the sill, taking me by surprise. Even as I gasp at the sudden violation of my peace, it struts, crying, and I exist in the now, the room taking substance round me.

I laugh, scramble to my feet, go across to pull faces at the gull. Beyond the window, the fog swirls. I am aware of the sound of the sea. Images flash through my brain. Red velvet turns to silver and palest green; upholstered chairs become unicorns tossing their manes like smoke upon the air – .

And then the sound of the Tyrolean cow-bell that hangs in the hall echoes through the house. Mrs Edwards is telling us that lunch is ready. I am ravenous. I run down the stairs while the bell still vibrates. I am alive and life is suddenly very good.

* * * *

Edwin is sitting at the round table in the dining-room. Dishes on the snowy cloth sizzle invitingly. The glasses and knives catch the grey light. The room is full of small rainbows, and I feel so bursting with power that I could catch them in my hands. Edwin holds out my chair, seats himself opposite to me. We smile at each other while we pile chops and vegetables onto the gold-rimmed plates.

"Well, have you finished your work?" Teasing him.

"Yes, pigeon, all done." His soft brown eyes rest on me with love. I look away hastily, beginning to eat.

"Did you write anything?" he asks.

"No, but I saw a sea-gull. It landed on the window-sill. It was a good idea to come here, wasn't it? Better than London. More elemental; you can feel the world turning."

Edwin chews his food thoughtfully, a slight frown between his brows. I try to repair the breach.

"I mean, you haven't cut yourself off completely. Just semi-retired. And the rest of the time you can relax. Not feel so pressured."

"No."

I want to tell him about the rainbows within the reach of my hands, the consciousness in this now, this moment, of El Dorado somewhere beyond the boom of the sea as the tide swirls below us, the glittering apples of the Hesperides lost in the mist outside the window. I can feel the longing to speak like a lump in my throat. I have difficultly in swallowing. I try to say something that will reach him.

"Shall we go for a walk after lunch, then?"

"If you would like to."

It is impossible. But I try again.

"I'm thinking of the flowers hidden under all this fog. The crocuses are coming out now, you know, they always remind me of jewels, so bright. The pink shrub's got loads of blossoms – I think it's an azalea – but they're white aren't they? – or it might be a camellia – oh, the romance of Marguerite Gautier – how lovely if we've got our own camellia – ."

Edwin grimaces suddenly.

"I'll have to tell Mrs Edwards to mash the potatoes in future, they're repeating on me."

I shut my eyes momentarily. When I open them, I look for the rainbows knowing they will be gone. El Dorado is an echo of old fables, dead men's tales from beyond the Pillars of Hercules. The Hesperides, shores of the Isles of the Blessed, were never there at all. The fog weeps outside the window.

I eat the food and taste nothing. My hands move stiffly, like those of an automaton. Edwin talks about share prices. I nod, a half-smile fixed to my mouth. The silver scrapes on the gold-rimmed plates.

"Edwin," I say desperately, "What day is it?"

"Wednesday, pigeon."

I'll hold onto Wednesday. And when we go for our walk, I know his hand will be there, his fingers gentle, possessive of mine. I'll have the stone flags of the path solid beneath my feet. The lilac bush by the gate will be dripping moisture. There's a road outside and the gulls will be calling.

I will ask Mrs Edwards for some bread. Give it to the gulls.

Look At Me Daddy – I'm Flying

BY DOREEN FIOL

"Father's dead!"

The words going round and around in her head didn't make sense, so she said them aloud.

"Father's dead. Father's dead."

She fumbled inside her mind for something to grasp, a sensible, rational thought to hold on to.

"Look at me Daddy, I'm flying!" Ah, that was it. She remembered the time. She had sat astride his shoulders, her ankles tucked under his armpits, and stretched her arms out. With gulls whirling and squabbling about them and the wind blowing her skirt up over her back she had felt delight, exhilaration. Seeing his shadow thrown against the rocks she had flapped her arms, making the gigantic, massive rock creature flap too.

"Look at me Daddy, I'm flying."

He can't be dead! For he had always been there; a large tyrannical, threatening, solid opposition to every thought, idea or dream she'd ever had – and yet needing her care, her love – and her protection.

Gradually the tension, the shut-in feeling that she had known all her life, started to lift. She felt like a bird sitting at the open door of its cage, sensing the space around but not yet knowing how to use it.

'A cup of tea' she thought. 'That's what I want. A nice strong cup of tea.'

Seated at the kitchen table, sipping her 'housewives panacea' as her mother used to call it, Phillipa's thoughts turned painfully backwards to when her mother was alive. Had it been worse then, or better because she had an ally? She didn't know. Both really. Worse because she had to see her mother suffer, watch her being gradually worn down, browbeaten, abused, physically and verbally, until she didn't really exist any more. Long before she had died, that terrible night two years ago when Phillipa had been just fifteen, she had died inside. Her last words to Phillipa had been "Get out darling – as soon as you can, get away . . ." Then, whispered, "Don't let him destroy you too – he doesn't mean it – he can't help himself."

And Phillipa had tried to get away.

At sixteen, instead of going to college as she had wanted she had got at job. 'As soon as I've saved up enough money for rent-in-advance and the deposit I'm going to get a bed-sit,' she had told herself. 'I can still pop round and look after Dad – I'll pick up my education again later.'

So she told herself, knowing it would never be.

Every time she had saved a little he had demanded help for some emergency; a crisis in the business (he worked for himself, doing up and selling old cars) a gambling debt – even a private nursing home bill!

He had had an ingrowing toe-nail for years but suddenly decided that it needed immediate attention.

"Can't afford the time off work to wait for the N.H.S. – they'll want several trips to their clinic and then a long wait for the operation," he'd explained, "Privately I can get it done when *I* want it."

So she had 'lent' him the money, as she always did, and, as always, it hadn't come back.

When, tentatively, she had mentioned it he had flown into one of his black rages, accusing her of being grasping and selfish – and of obtaining the money by 'whoring' in the first place! She hadn't mentioned it again, but the next time he asked for a 'loan' she had lied, saying she hadn't any money. She shuddered as she remembered his anger – she had never seen him so angry.

She should have known better. She'd never been any good at lying.

It had been several days before she could get to the 'phone box to telephone them at work, (her father would not allow a 'phone in the house, only in his workshop.) She could not produce a doctor's certificate this time – he would never believe she had fallen downstairs again.

Her job was no longer open, she was told. They had taken on someone more reliable.

Why had she stayed? Why had she not told somebody? Probably for the same reasons as her mother had tolerated the intolerable. Because, as her mother had, she loved him.

She could hear her mother's voice now – "Don't tell anyone Daddy hit me, love, – they won't understand – he doesn't mean it," and many, many times, "Don't cry love, Daddy didn't mean to hurt you – he loves you really."

There it was. 'Daddy loves you really.'

Waiting, waiting – always waiting and hoping for one little sign, for something, other than her mother's words, to tell her that, really, he did love her.

Oh, how she had wanted him to love her!

As a tiny child she would try so hard to please him. How many times when her mother said "Goodnight" she would ask "Have I been good?" "Of course you've been good, Poppet – an Angel."

"You will tell Daddy won't you?"

"Yes, love, I'll tell him – soon as he comes in."

And again, as her mother reached the door, "Mummy – don't forget to tell Daddy I've been good."

But she was rarely good enough.

When her father was home everything that went wrong, from business to the weather, seemed to be the fault of one small girl, and of course, her mother. If they spoke they were disturbing him; if they were quiet they were sulking and discontented – implying criticism of him. If they laughed together, or played a game they were shutting him out. His wife, asking him a question, was prying. Not asking him anything was disinterest. His daughter, trying to tell him about school, friends, a book, a toy, was prattling and bothering him with trivialities. So she stopped trying to talk to him, just watched him dumbly – and was stupid.

Except sometimes. Sometimes she was his Princess, his clever little girl, his joy, and he would caress her, and play with her. Like that day on the beach.

But only sometimes. Rarely. Sometimes. The occasions becoming less frequent with the years.

She remembered, a long time ago it seemed, her mother being happy and lively when they were alone together, the shadow only coming over them when Father came home. But gradually the oppression which hung over them like a living monster stretched its tentacles into every corner of their daily life until nothing was untouched by it. Her mother, who at one time would chat to neighbours while shopping, would hurry past with the briefest of nods, nervous of the row she would cause if she delayed. A long queue at the check-out could mean days of criticism, with Father walking around the house, checking corners for dust, complaining about the cooking, finding creases in his shirts and finally exploding in a tirade of abuse aimed at them both – her mother for not doing her job properly and Phillipa for being born.

So they had tried harder to please him.

"He's under a lot of pressure," her mother would say. "We must try to humour him," and the inevitable, "He doesn't mean it – he loves us really."

They did so want it to be true. And sometimes – it *was* true.

As she grew up she watched him, wondering why he was so different from other girls' fathers. She knew from school that children went to each other's homes, that mothers went out visiting and to the cinema and had friends – and even went to work.

She had been invited to other girls' homes – they seemed to like her at school – but had not been allowed to go.

"You'll mix up with the wrong sort," her father had said. She had told him he could meet them first if he liked, but he had replied that he had something better to do with his time than waste it socialising with morons – and it was a pity she hadn't too. Two school friends did call at the house once, but he was so unpleasant to them they never called again. Phillipa, apologising for him, had explained to them that she had upset him and he was still angry when they called. The sort of explanation her mother always gave for his ill-humour.

Yet he was not always bad-tempered. The two men who worked with him thought he was a 'smashing bloke' – good to work for and very fair – she'd heard them say so. And if she went to his workshop in the yard with a message, or his lunch, he always greeted her as if he was proud of her and would smile and put an arm around her. Her mother too would be spoken to civilly and even affectionately, although she never saw him touch her, except in anger, in private.

But once back home it took so little to trigger off a change of mood. Sometimes they would try for days to think what they had said or done, each assuming they must have been to blame, each reassuring the other.

It was during her mother's last, terrible illness that Phillipa had first realized her father was sick. Not just difficult and unpredictable, but really sick. With the cancer taking her last physical energy her mother had seemed to acquire some inner strength and gained in stature as she became dwarfed by the ravages of the disease. One day when her father had started his usual complaining about her 'lying around feeling sorry for herself while he was expected to do the skivvying' (he had ironed his own shirt as Phillipa had not done it to his satisfaction) she had turned to him, all eyes in her grey, sunken face, and said, almost angrily, "Face up to life Len – I'm going beyond your reach – you can't hurt me anymore. And what'll you do without a punch-bag? Don't think Phillipa will let you take it out on her forever. She'll think for herself sooner or later."

Phillipa had held her breath, expecting him to hit out, punch, smash up the room. But he hadn't. He had stopped, looked at her long and deep, as if seeing her for the first time, and sunk slowly to his knees beside the bed, and cried. And how he had cried! Deep, terrible sobs, ugly and terrifying. And through the sobs his voice as Phillipa had never heard it before, not harsh and frightening, but weak and whining and pitiful.

"Jeannie, don't leave me – please – I'll never hurt you again – I'm sorry – I don't know what gets into me – I don't mean it – I'm so full of hate – but it's not you I hate, nor Phillipa – it's me – it's me. I wish I was dead – I should be dead – then I couldn't hurt anyone anymore. Don't die Jeannie. Don't die. Don't leave me."

And all the time those hideous, rasping sobs.

Her mother's hand had rested, briefly, on his head, then she had turned away and beckoned Phillipa. It was then that she had spoken her last words, at the end barely audible.

Slipping into a coma she had died during the night.

For a week her father had not spoken except to make arrangements for the cremation. Her mother had some relatives whom she had not seen for some years but with whom she had kept in touch by letter. Phillipa had been given the task of inviting them to the funeral. That, cleaning the house and preparing a buffet meal, had been left to her. Her father had organised everything else quietly and efficiently with the minimum of communications. She was, therefore, surprised at the funeral at how well he coped with the well-meaning but meaningless small talk, so integral a part of these occasions when strangers are making a pretence of belonging.

But his grief was genuine, and it showed.

"It's all right Mum," she had thought to herself, "You needn't have worried about us – he's going to be different now – he did love you really, as you've always said, and me too. He won't go back to being how he was."

But he did – immediately their guests had gone Phillipa had been blazed into the terrible awareness that nothing had changed – except that she no longer had her mother.

Phillipa poured herself another cup of tea – cold now, but she didn't notice – and returned to her reflections.

After losing her job a boy she had worked with had called round. Thank goodness her father was at work! She was flustered and panic-stricken.

"Look – it's nice of you to call – I'll go shopping. Meet you in the cafe – you know – where we went for lunch."

"Why can't I come in and talk – you don't look fit to go out."

She had forgotten the bruises and the split lip – what a mess she must look!

"Whatever did you do anyway? Walk into a bus?" He was concerned, solicitous.

"No – I – I fell downstairs."

"Again? You did that last time you were off work – so you said."

"Yea. No." She fumbled for ideas, reasons, "I don't want to talk about it" she finished lamely.

Then Phillipa's eyes widened. Horrified she watched her father coming along the path.

"Oh go – please go . . ."

He turned to see what was distressing her – it was obvious she was afraid. Before he could say a word he was pushed roughly aside and Phillipa was being shaken like a rag doll.

"Bitch! Whore! This is what you're up to while I'm at work – slaving to keep a slut! A nice daughter for a man to have! No wonder your poor mother died with the worry you've given her, knowing what you're like."

Turning to the boy who was trying to pull him away from Phillipa he roared

"Get out – Get out you dirty bastard – sniffing round my girl as if she's a bitch on heat – even if that's what she is – Get out!"

Phillipa looked at the boy through rapidly closing eyes.

"Go Jerry" she said quietly.

"I'm getting the Police."

"No!" She was emphatic. "I'll deal with this. Just go please."

He had gone, hesitantly, doubtfully, not knowing what he should do.

She had met him secretly after that, frequently, but never for long. And for the first time she had talked about her father.

"You should have him put away," Jerry had said.

"I can't" she had replied. "He's my father – and he doesn't mean it. Deep down he loves me."

"Funny way of showing it." Jerry had a very simple, direct attitude towards life. "Try to get him to see a shrink – he's a nut-case."

She had tried, tactfully to suggest to her father that maybe he needed help.

Not tactfully enough, however, as her next 'fall downstairs' had proved.

"It's no use Jerry, I can't leave him – he needs me – he's scared of being left alone – I found that out when my mother died. And I can't report him – he might go to prison – or worse. He couldn't stand being locked up – and he wouldn't stay – prison or hospital or anywhere if they didn't. And anyway – he doesn't mean it – he's always so sorry after."

As indeed he was. Sometimes he would come quietly to her room, knocking almost timidly, and ask her to come down for a little chat. Then he would let her know how sorry he was, in that sad, unusual voice, and he would cry. She'd be embarrassed then and try to comfort him.

"It's alright Dad – really – I know you don't mean it."

"Well, you can't go on like this," Jerry broke in to her thoughts.

"No, you're right Jerry, I can't." She had answered. She went to the window and looked out. Yes, there was Jerry by the 'phone box looking for her signal. She drew one curtain across. He would walk past the house now, at the back, and she would normally run to catch him up. But not today. She opened the back door.

"Jerry," she called "Jerry."

He came, somewhat hesitantly toward her. Seeing the blood spattered all over her he started to run to her.

"Oh my God – Phillipa – What has he done?"

"It's alright Jerry," she moved back inside, stepping carefully over the body so that Jerry could enter.

"He hasn't done anything . . . he nearly did, but I took it off him – I know he didn't want to really – so I stopped him – to help him. Don't you see? I had to help him – my Daddy doesn't like to hurt people really – he's always so sorry after – and I don't like to see him cry."

Jerry saw each detail clearly but nothing made sense, nothing knitted together. The details were all so separate. The pointed, very sharp kitchen knife with its burnt handle, kept, in spite of the damage, for its all-purpose usefulness; the tea-cup and pot beside it, the milk still in the bottle, the fridge door not quite closed properly – he was aware of the whirring noise the fridge makes trying to cool itself. He saw the large mass at his feet and Phillipa, the blood on her hands and face dry now, but still moist on her clothing. He wanted to move, to understand, to run, to be sick. He wondered why his feet felt glued to the floor. Looking down he saw the sticky mess holding them. Then the desire to be sick overcame all else and he swayed putting his hand out to the back of a chair to steady himself. The chair was sticky too. He took his hand hurriedly away and almost fell.

Helping him to the sink Phillipa moved the washing-up bowl out of his way on to the draining board, picking up the cup and the knife and adding them to the still unwashed breakfast things as she did so. Seeing him still retching and heaving she put an arm round him sympathetically.

"It's alright Jerry. My Daddy won't grumble at you for making a mess – Daddy's gone away."

They locked the door to the ward carefully, not looking at her as she walked between them along the long green and cream corridor, talking across her as if she wasn't there. They had got used to not watching her – she never moved unless she was taken somewhere; to the table, to bed, to the recreation room, or, as now, to the psychiatrist's room. She had no interest in anything now, with Daddy gone. Where had he gone? Oh – that's right – to Heaven – up in the sky with Jesus – That's what they'd told her at school when she was little. But how had he got up there? She glanced briefly at a window, not barred as she was used to. Nice. You could see more sky.

It's high up there – a long way up. Of course – he'd flown. How else? Once he nearly taught her how to fly.

The next window, the French kind, opened on to a small balcony overlooking the well-kept grounds. Again, as they drew level she glanced that way. A long way down people were walking about on their own, but that didn't interest her. Two off-duty attendants were seated on office chairs to one side of the balcony enjoying the early spring sunshine. One was reading, the other picking at a toe-nail. She thought, momentarily, that she knew something about a toe-nail, but she couldn't remember what. It didn't matter anyway.

They had all got used to not watching her.

"She was so quick," they said, later, "There was nothing we could do."

As she stood briefly, balanced on the edge, she looked up, spreading her arms wide.

"Look at me Daddy, I'm flying."

Notes on Contributors

The contributors have supplied the following notes about themselves

BETTY BEYER: Born in Newport, South Wales, with an English mother and Canadian father. Left school at sixteen, moved to Bristol and then London. Married, brought up three children. Worked in public libraries. During the seventies spent summers in Canada, winters in Cornwall. In 1985/6 was a student at Fircroft Adult College in Birmingham. Returned to Cornwall permanently in 1986.

PEARL CARRINGTON was born in the Midlands, but has lived and worked as a hotelier and publican in Cornwall for many years. Now retired, she lives in the beautiful village of St Mawgan in Pydar and spends her time writing, knitting and singing in the choir.

GARY COUZENS was born in 1964 and read English at the University of Southampton. He has written film reviews and articles for *Due South* and *Thameswey News*. *Drowning* is the second short story he has had accepted, the first being *Loving*; he has just completed a novel. He lives in Aldershot and works for British Telecom.

DOREEN FIOL was born in London in 1931 and now lives in Cornwall with her husband. Mother of seven children, a trained nurse and President of the Lanner Writers' Group, she has written for newspapers and magazines, completed two children's books and many Children's Theatre productions. She is currently working on a novel.

PATRICIA FRAZER: I live in Shrewsbury with my husband and two cats. Other interests include walking, church interests and gardening. My parents live in Looe, and I return to visit Cornwall frequently. I have been writing for most of my life, poetry and short stories mainly, but have also had articles published in magazines.

DILYS GATOR's twenty-year career as a writer has covered broadcasting, journalism and full-length work both fiction and non-fiction. She has written over fifty books, many of which have appeared all over the world. She has been a tutor for two writing schools and written many articles on how to write. She lives in London.

GILL GRIBBLE: Born in Surrey in 1957, Gill moved to Cornwall six years later, living in Helston and Bodmin. After graduating from Plymouth Polytechnic she spent time in Botswana and Ireland, returning to Cornwall in 1982. A part-time art student, Gill has written poetry and stories for many years. She is married with three daughters.

GLADYS HARVEY: A potted biography – simple unfortunately. Born Plymouth, lived in Penzance since childhood, always scribbling. Why didn't I do something interesting like walking round the world backwards, or even a piffling little parachute jump? Well, I didn't know I was going to be asked for my biography, did I? My age? Naff off!

(The irrepressible Gladys, of uncertain age, has broadcast a morning short story and other pieces for radio and has had short stories published in *Bella*, *Best*, *Woman's Realm* and *My Weekly* as well as having work published in the *London Evening News*. Her secret? Naff off! *Editor*.)

HARVEY KURZFIELD is a primary school teacher and lives in Redruth. He has been writing, on and off, for years and years – though mainly for pleasure. For the last four years he has been the Secretary of the Lanner Writers' Group and in 1990 won their short story competition. Recently he completed his first children's novel. His other interests include drama and music.

JANET ROSALIE MOODIE is a writer and textile artist. Originally from Yorkshire she studied textiles at the Royal College of Art. After living and working in London for thirty years, Janet now lives at Godolphin, where she is working on her second novel and creating woven textiles.

DAVID NUTT: Born in Easton, Bristol. As a child and teenager was always preoccupied with writing and the visual arts. Written twenty short stories; some published, some winning minor literary awards. Ninety-one poems, many of which have been published, some awarded. Three novels written, two of which are being revised currently. A member of Clifton Arts Club and a long-standing member of the West Country Writers' Association.

ROY PHILLIPS was born in St Ives and has lived in west Cornwall since, apart from National Service in the Far East and travels in the Middle East and Central Asia. He is a Bard of the Cornish Gorsedd and won the Winston Churchill Travelling Fellowship in 1979. He has written widely on ornithology and in 1987 he won the prestigious TSB Peninsula prize with his acclaimed first novel *The Saffron Eaters*.

LUCY SPEAR was born in London. She is married to a Cornishman and lives in Flushing, near Falmouth. She has been writing stories and poems for pleasure since childhood, but has only considered writing for publication since the births of her two children.

JOHN T WILSON has been writing since his first publication in a school magazine at the age of ten. His work has been widely published in a variety of magazines and journals and he has published half a dozen short non-fiction books. Formerly Principal of a large Adult Education Centre in the south east he now lives in Cornwall where he runs his own small publishing house and edits and publishes *Freelance Writing and Photography* magazine.